"Will you let m̲.̲.̲.̲.̲ ̲y̲.̲.̲,̲ ̲J̲e̲s̲s̲?̲"

King gathered Jesse in a gentle but fierce embrace. "I've got you now, honey. And I swear to God, no one will ever hurt you again. Do you hear me? No one!"

Jesse let herself absorb the essence of this man...her King. Once he'd been her world.

For the first time since her attack, Jesse believed she would survive. She wasn't alone now. King wouldn't let anyone hurt her again. She believed that as surely as she knew the sun would rise each day.

* * *

"Ms. Sala tugs at our heartstrings with tender persistence, making us ache with joy and wonder."

—*Romantic Times Magazine*

"Sharon Sala is not only a top romance novelist, she is an inspiration for people everywhere who wish to live their dreams."

—John St. Augustine, Power! Talk Radio
WDBC-AM Michigan

Dear Reader,

I must thank Silhouette for giving me the chance to share this story with you again. Oddly enough, this book, which is my second published book, was the most difficult story I ever had to write.

The prologue of *King's Ransom* is loosely based on something that really happened to my youngest child, my daughter Kathryn, but the kidnapping and the rest of the story are fiction. It took me longer to write those first few pages than it did the entire rest of the book. The pain, rage and helplessness of knowing someone tried to murder your child is something I pray none of you ever have to know. Suffice it to say, my daughter survived and the man who committed the crime is sitting on death row in an Oklahoma penitentiary.

As you read this book, know that there are valiant, courageous people all over the world who are victimized, but who find a power within themselves not to be victims. Today, Kathryn teaches four-year-old children in the Oklahoma public school system, and she is a true heroine in real life. When you read this story, think of her.

I love to hear from my readers. I can be reached at P.O. Box 127, Henryetta, OK, 74437.

Sharon Sala

SHARON SALA

KING'S RANSOM

Published by Silhouette Books

America's Publisher of Contemporary Romance

SILHOUETTE BOOKS

ISBN 0-373-48421-6

KING'S RANSOM

Copyright © 1992 by Sharon Sala.

First published by Meteor Publishing Corporation.

For Kathryn, who suffered, endured and prevailed

Chapter 1

A fetid smell, an odor of liquor, rough ugly words, and promises of what he was going to do filtered through Jesse's exhausted sleep. She heard a deep, rasping breath and knew it was not her own. Her heart stopped.

He knew the moment she awoke, because he clamped his hand loosely over her face, pinching her mouth and cheeks, pushed the knife point against her throat, and told her not to scream.

It was the wrong thing to say to Jesse LeBeau. She had never liked being told what to do. Her terrified scream erupted into the menacing silence of the room and later Jesse would remember thinking, *tonight I'm going to die!*

His anger was evident as he growled an ugly threat

and began to face what he had unwittingly unleashed. This wasn't the way it was meant to happen.

Jesse fought like a woman possessed as her constant screams and fierce struggle for possession of the knife threw the intruder into a frenzy.

He felt the girl's fingernails catch deep into the flesh of his cheekbone and rake the entire length of his jaw. He lost control of his emotions and the situation entirely, forgetting, in his fury, why he'd ever entered her house.

"Bitch!" he yelled, and thrust downward over and over with the knife, only to connect with air or bedclothes. He struggled, trying to gain control of her flailing fists, and blanched as her knee connected with a tender part of his anatomy. That was all she was going to do to him. He would have no more of this catwoman. He raised the knife upward once again and suddenly his hand come away empty.

There was no time for surprise as he felt the first thrust of the knife right above his shoulder blade. His wild shriek of pain only added to the confusion going on in his head. This wasn't the way he'd planned any of this. Now he was on the defensive and fear overrode all his other emotions. He struck out wildly with doubled fists, trying to connect with the source of those damnable screams, but the ear-splitting sound of the woman's fear and rage, and the constant pain in his chest and back were more than he could bear. He moaned softly and slumped forward heavily.

Unaware of his near unconscious condition, Jesse

continued to stab blindly at his dead weight as it forced her deeper and deeper into her mattress.

Suddenly she was free! Somehow she'd managed to roll his still body aside. She crawled from the bed on hands and knees, still clutching the knife, still screaming. She ran on fear, unaware her attacker was not moving, imagining she could feel his hand on her shoulder as she dashed from her home in St. Louis and into the street. Her screams had alerted the entire block of her neighborhood, and she was vaguely aware of lights coming on in one house and then another. But no one came out to help her.

It was the scream of the siren from the police car flying around the street corner that silenced Jesse. The psychedelic whirl of red and blue lights momentarily disoriented her and she staggered as it came to a screeching halt only inches from where she stood.

"Lady, drop the knife," the policeman ordered, as he stood with gun drawn behind the open door of his cruiser, uncertain about what kind of situation he was facing. All he could see was a very bloody woman with an oversized butcher knife.

"Please," Jesse begged, and started forward, unaware of the picture she presented with blood-covered night clothes and a knife in her hand.

The policeman took a deep breath and ordered again, in a much louder voice.

"I said, drop the knife!"

Jesse looked stunned. What had happened to her

world? She looked at the policeman's face, the gun in his hand, and slumped to her knees on the pavement.

"Here," she whispered, and laid the knife on the ground in front of her. "Now will you help me?"

"Jesus, Captain!" the officer said, as they carefully walked through the house where the attack had taken place. "Look at all this blood. Looks like someone was butcherin' a hog. And here," he continued, as he pointed toward Jesse's bedroom window, careful not to touch anything as the crime lab crew continued their sweep of the premises. "The bastard crawled out of the bedroom window, probably when the girl ran for help." The streaks and smeared blood on the wall and windowsill made the man's exit point easy to read.

Captain Shockey was four years shy of retirement, short and overweight, a nondescript individual with a mind like a NASA computer. He could read a crime scene like a trucker reads a map. And it had been a long time since he'd seen anything like this disaster. This was a decent, family-oriented neighborhood, a comfortable, but unpretentious house. The victim was an elementary school teacher, and obviously meticulously neat. The bedroom looked like what he'd seen in Vietnam. Blood was on the walls near the window in an obvious spray pattern. He was guessing the girl had nicked one of the attacker's veins. The bedclothes were torn from the bed, slash marks and pools of blood had seeped into the mattress. Bloody footprints went in two directions. The larger ones, wearing shoes, had staggered toward the window, the smaller, bare footprints were widely spaced, and led toward the hallway the girl had used to get out of the house.

Shockey could tell by the distance between the little bare prints that the girl had been moving very fast. Hell, he would have been, too. How she had survived anything like this was beyond his comprehension. He knew his next stop would have to be the hospital to question the victim. He hated that part of the job because all it did was make them relive the terror. But it was necessary if he was going to catch the nut who'd done this.

"Is she in any shape to talk?" he asked the officer.

"Yes, sir," he answered, as he stepped aside to let the photographer get a better shot of the bed and window. "I never saw anything like her. She's not very big, can't be more than three or four inches over five feet, but she's all fire, and until we catch this guy, I don't think her fire's goin' out. When I was talkin' to her earlier, I felt like I was the one being questioned." He grinned slightly at the captain's raised eyebrows and sardonic expression. "Also, I didn't see too many deep cuts on her, except for her hands. They looked bad. I think most of the blood on her belonged to the perpetrator. Hell," he said, then swallowed hard as he looked away from the sharp gaze of Captain Shockey. "She took that knife away with her bare hands. I don't know if I'd have had the guts to do something like that."

Shockey patted the young officer on the back—a rough, locker room pat—and answered.

"You never know what you're capable of, boy, until you face the wall. Check and see if there're any family or next-of-kin to notify. She's going to need all the moral support she can get. Come on, get cracking," he urged. "We've got us a real bad one to catch this time. Maybe we'll get lucky and find him dead. From the looks of this place, it's possible."

"Yes, sir," the officer answered, and watched Shockey rumble between the lab crew, side-stepping them like he was dodging fresh cow patties. If anyone could find the perpetrator, Shockey was the man for the job.

The sharp, persistent ring finally penetrated King McCandless's deep sleep, and he rolled over in bed, taking a wad of bedclothes with him, as he fumbled for the clock. Then he realized it wasn't the alarm after all; it was the phone. A deep, pulling sensation in the pit of his stomach brought him fully awake as he turned on the lamp and saw the green digital numbers on his clock. Nearly four in the morning. Not the time for good news. Rolling over to a sitting position, he let his long, pajama-clad legs brace him as he grabbed the phone in the middle of another ring. Taking a long, slow breath, he let his deep, raspy voice break the silence.

"Hello?" As he heard the male voice and the authority behind it, he shuddered unconsciously. It reminded him of the call he'd received when his father, Andrew McCandless, had died. "Yes, this is King McCandless."

He didn't see his bedroom door open, or see the worried expression on the face of his housekeeper, Maggie West, as she shakily tied her robe around her plump stomach. Her long, gray braid hung over her shoulder and she pulled at it nervously as she watched King take the call.

Maggie's heart caught in her throat. She saw the blood drain from King's face. It *was* bad news! She knew it. No good ever came of a phone ringing this time of the morning. She watched him nod, and repeat and address back to the person at the other end of the call.

King slowly laid the phone in its cradle and buried his head in his hands, unaware of Maggie's presence.

"What?" she asked, assured of her right to know by her almost twenty years of service to the McCandless family. Her frantic tone of voice startled King.

He turned, saw Maggie's worried face, and had to swallow twice before he could speak aloud the horror he'd just absorbed.

"It's Jesse," he whispered, and then had to clear his throat before he could continue. "Someone tried to kill her."

"Merciful God in heaven. Is she…is she hurt bad?"

Maggie couldn't stop the free flow of tears that sprang to her eyes. She'd put in ten years raising that child, too, even if she wasn't a McCandless.

Mike LeBeau and Andrew McCandless had been
partners in the early 1960s and 1970s during an
Oklahoma oil boom. When Mike had been killed on a
drilling rig during an ice storm, Andrew had become
Jesse's guardian. She had only been twelve. Jesse was
absorbed into the McCandless clan like she'd been
born into it and she'd stayed happily, until two years
after Andrew McCandless's death. Then, for reasons
known only to Jesse, she had quietly taken a job in St.
Louis, Missouri, and never come back. They still kept
in touch, but she'd gently refused all their invitations
to visit.

In answer to Maggie's question regarding Jesse's
condition, King had to consider his words before he
spoke. She couldn't be in the hospital and be okay, but
he didn't know any details.

"I just don't know, Maggie," King said, as he
yanked the bedclothes away from his long legs with a
jerk. "But I'm damn sure going to find out. Help me
pack, will you? Don't skimp on clothes. I don't know
how long I'll stay. I just know I won't be back without
her."

Maggie's nod of approval went unnoticed as King
grabbed the nearest pair of jeans from his closet and
headed for the dressing area of his bathroom.

Relieved that there was something positive she could
do, Maggie began emptying drawers of freshly laun-
dered underwear, shirts, and socks into an oversized
suitcase that King pulled from a hall closet. Between
the two of them, King was dressed, packed, and on his

way to Tulsa and the airport within the hour. If he was lucky, he should just about make the next flight.

Steam was rising from the pavement as he pulled his car into a parking garage at the airport. It was already above 85 degrees and no relief from the mid-July temperatures in Oklahoma was expected.

"Gonna be another hot one," the parking attendant said, as he would to everyone he waited on that day. "Gonna park her long?" he asked, eyeing the opulence of the shiny black Lincoln.

"I have no idea." King fixed a hard, dark stare on the attendant. "But I expect it to be here when I get back."

"No problem. No problem with that at all, just so's you have the parkin' stub. Know what I mean? Can't be givin' these babies away to just anybody. No sirree!"

King was distracted. He could have cared less about the car and allowed the attendant's spiel to flow over him unheard.

A trickle of perspiration ran slowly down his back as he raced to the ticket counter just in time to get his boarding pass. He wondered if the sweat was from the heat or from fear. Damn it all to hell and back, he hated to fly. He grimaced, took his assigned seat, and knew that only Jesse's predicament could have persuaded him to use this method of travel. All he was concerned with was getting to her as quickly as possible.

An anonymous blue van was parked under the overhanging branches of a huge sugar maple. The motor was quiet, but no one would have noticed it anyway. Nearly every house in the area was shut tightly against the heat, with air conditioners going full blast. It was always hot this time of year, even at night, and no one was ready to lose sleep for a few dollars' worth of electricity. Maybe later when they received their costly utility bills, but not yet. This was the reason no one saw a man staggering through the shrubbery, trying to make his way toward the van. And the houses were far enough away from Jesse's that they wouldn't have heard her screams for help.

The man in the bushes was following the sound of the van's running motor. He was so blinded by the pain in his chest and back he could barely focus. The clumsy duffle bag he was dragging behind him kept getting hung in the thick bushes.

The driver fidgeted, glanced several times at the luminous dial on his watch, and knew it was taking far too long. How much time could it possibly take to subdue one very small woman, tie and blindfold her, and carry her less than a block through the alley?

Just as he had started to exit the van to investigate, a police siren broke the silence of the night, and he nearly fell from the van door. When he caught himself, he also thought he could hear a woman screaming for help. Jesus Christ! he thought. *I should have known that fool couldn't pull this off.* Instinct told him to leave, but he knew if the idiot was caught, he would be implicated in an instant.

His meandering panic was interrupted. His heart thudded to an abrupt halt as he saw the stooped figure stumbling about in the hedge bordering the alleyway. He dashed toward him, thinking he would help carry the girl.

"Oh hell! Oh hell!" the man moaned, as he fell into the driver's outstretched arms. "Get me out of here."

"Where's the girl?" the driver snarled, and grabbed hard at the man's arm.

"Aieee," he shrieked, and then staggered backwards in pain. "I didn't get her. But she hurt me. She hurt me bad. You've got to get me out of here and get me some help. I'm bleeding to death."

A long string of curses erupted from the driver's mouth as he saw the blood. It was everywhere. The fool was covered in it, and even worse, had gotten it on him, too. Enraged, he shoved the wounded man toward the van, slid the side door open and shoved him and the duffle bag roughly toward the gaping hole. He slammed the door shut, not caring whether the man was completely clear of the door's force. Hurrying to the driver's side, he quickly concealed himself from any curious eyes. For two cents he'd finish the job the girl started and leave the fool for the street sweepers. But he didn't. He was a careful man and decided to dispose of this garbage in his own way.

"What in hell happened?" the driver snarled, as he turned up the opposite alley, driving as quickly as possible without alerting the neighborhood. It was only after he'd gone several blocks and turned onto a main thoroughfare that he'd turned on his headlights. "Can't you do anything right, Lynch? You owed me, and this botched episode does not cancel anything. Do you hear me?"

"Jesus, I'm hurt bad. You got to get me to a doctor. And it ain't my fault things didn't go right. You didn't tell me what she was like. Dammit, man, I could have stuffed a tiger in a gunny sack easier than this. Hell," he groaned, slumping lower into the seat he'd pulled himself into, "she shouldn't have fought me. She made me mad."

"What do you mean?" the driver asked in a menacing whisper. "You didn't hurt her did you? This blood all better be yours. You weren't supposed to kill her, just kidnap her. Answer me! Is she hurt?"

"To hell with her," he whined. "Just look at me. I'll have scars for life, if I don't bleed to death."

"You tell me now," the driver snarled, and slammed the van to a screeching halt in the middle of a deserted street, "or I swear to God, I'll finish what she started."

It was obvious to the injured man that his condition was less than important. He should have known not to get mixed up in something like this anyway.

"She ain't hurt hardly at all. Just a few scratches. I wasn't trying to kill her," he whined, and felt himself losing a grip on reality. "She just made me mad, that's all. Now please, get me some help!"

For a few moments, the van remained motionless. Then it accelerated slowly, as if the driver couldn't quite decide what he was going to do. Finally it picked up speed and disappeared into the darkness.

Jesse had adamantly refused any kind of anesthetic that would render her unconscious. She wasn't about to be put to sleep. The last time she slept, someone tried to kill her. She wasn't going through that again.

She welcomed the roughness of the warm, wet wash-cloth on her face. She knew the nurse was being as gentle as she could as she washed away the ugly traces of her ordeal.

As the bloodstains disappeared, the fragile beauty of the young woman appeared—a heart-shaped face, thick, dark wavy hair just below shoulder length, and wide, sky-blue eyes above a near perfect nose with just the tiniest inclination to tilt. But there was no happiness to pull her soft, generous mouth into its usual smile. Jesse LeBeau was trying hard not to lose her mind and the only way she knew for certain she could do that was to avoid being put back to sleep.

"Okay, little lady," the doctor said, acquiescing to Jesse's demands for only local pain-killers. "There isn't that much to put back together. I think you can take it. After all, you're a real toughie, aren't you?" He kept up his banter, trying to take Jesse's mind off the actual act of minor surgery that he was going to perform on her hands. "And, I do understand...okay?"

"Okay," Jesse whispered on a shaky sigh of relief, and allowed herself to relax momentarily. "Just re-member you promised." Her chin wobbled a bit as she struggled with the urge to scream and scream and never stop. "My students at Lee Elementary wouldn't break a promise to me, so you can't either."

Jesse managed a slight smile and then took a deep breath as the first needle full of the pain-killing solution entered the shredded area of her hand.

It took longer than expected, but she managed to stay alert as they worked. It was only after she was in her assigned room, groggy from all the drugs they'd shot into her system, that she'd let down her defenses and dozed off. Then the medicine kept her lethargic enough that she couldn't pull herself from the somnambulant state. She hung, suspended in a world of nightmares, where, as she had feared, she relived her attack over... and over...and over.

The elevator door opened as one lone passenger emerged. He stood unmoving, silently assessing the lay of Garrison Memorial Hospital's second floor. He was just recovering from the tension of the flight. He'd had to find a hotel and deposit his luggage, when all he wanted to do was get to Jesse. He'd let his imagination run to all sorts of horror but felt that the sooner he saw Jesse for himself, the better he was going to feel.

Loud talking, telephones ringing, and carts being shuffled about alerted King to the location of the nurses' station. He started down the long corridor, his nostrils twitching as he recognized the familiar smells of hospital disinfectant, the faint but unmistakable scents of flowers in the various rooms, and always, in spite of the constant antiseptic cleaning, the smell of sickness and dying. His muscular legs covered the distance quickly.

Several of the nurses watched his approach with more than usual interest.

"Look at that!" one of them whispered. "Don't you love it? Boots, jeans, sexy walk, and all."

"Yes," the other nurse answered. "I'm sort of partial to those slim hips, broad shoulders, and that big old cowboy hat. Makes me wish I'd been born about a hundred years ago."

"What do you need with a hundred years ago, dummy? Right there comes the civilized version of your dream."

"Well," she drawled, as King came closer, "I don't want them too civilized, if you know what I mean." And then she whispered, as King came closer, anxious that her words not be overheard, "Ooh, is there no justice? He's got that lean, hungry look, too."

She was referring to the chiseled planes of King's face. They were distinctive features inherited from his Scottish ancestors. The high cheekbones, shapely nose, once broken and nearly mended as good as new, a strong, stubborn chin and full, yet firm lips that were capable of a sardonic or sensual twist, depending on his quicksilver mood. Dark hair and dark eyes were the only features he had inherited from his mother's side of the family. His sport coat was draped casually across his arm in deference to the heat and humidity beyond the air-conditioned corridors of the hospital. The heat

King was generating at the nurses' station had nothing
to do with the outside temperatures. His appearance
was stunning, but he really got their attention when he
asked for their latest patient.

King spoke even before he came to a complete stop.
His voice was deep and raspy, a voice women always
found incredibly sexy. It was actually the result of riding into a low-hanging clothesline on a horse—in the
dark.

He had been celebrating his eighteenth birthday in a
most unsatisfactory manner, as his father often reminded him over the ensuing weeks. He'd been a bit
drunk. He knew never to drink and drive, but no one
told him not to drink and ride. They didn't have to tell
him again after his accident. He hadn't been able to
talk for a month, and when he finally could, the husky
rasp was all that was left of his voice. That was the
last time he ever rode a horse full tilt in the dark, and
the last time he ever got drunk. King McCandless was
not a fool twice.

"Jesse LeBeau," he asked, "what room please?"

The RN on duty stepped out of her cubicle as she
heard the name of their incognito patient. They had
been instructed by the police to check every visitor
asking about the young attack victim.

King's dark eyes followed the woman who stepped
up to the desk to answer his question.

"What business do you have with her?" she asked
crisply.

"Listen, lady," King answered, "I got a phone call

about four o'clock this morning that probably took ten years off my life and I've been on a damn plane ever since, trying to get here to Jesse. Now can you tell me where she is, or do I have to go find her myself?''

The nurse knew rope when she saw it, and this man was just about at the end of his. She came around the desk and motioned for him to follow.

''She's down at the end of the hall. Room 202. It's a single, makes it easier to maintain security, and there's an officer at the door. You have to get past him. And your name had better be on his list or threats won't make a whistle-stop worth of difference.''

Her sardonic tone was not lost on King, and he turned his head sharply, eyeing the nurse with new-found respect and a silent look of apology. He smiled slightly as he saw her accept. Sure enough, it took several pieces of identification proving he was actually who he claimed to be before the guard would allow him inside.

He hesitated, suddenly afraid of what he might see when he opened the door. But his hesitation disappeared when he heard the soft, agonizing moans and mumbled cries for help. King took one frantic look at the guard. He answered with a grimace and a shrug. He was helpless to stop what was going on behind the closed doors, too.

''She's just dreaming, Mr. McCandless. It's been going on for hours.''

King muttered under his breath as he shoved his way past the guard and entered the room. It was obvious

Jesse's agitation had been going on for some time. The bedclothes were in a wadded mess. The high, chrome guard rails were in place to keep Jesse from rolling out of the bed, but she had bunched herself completely against the back of one, trying in sleepy desperation to escape her attacker.

King couldn't describe the emotion that overwhelmed him as he witnessed the terror she was living. His first instinct was to awaken her, get her to see she was no longer in danger; but something made him hesitate. He didn't want to frighten her more. A cold rage filled his mind, and he knew, if he ever had the chance to do anything about it, the man responsible for her injuries and terror would know far worse before King was through with him.

He took his sport coat off his arm and laid it across the foot of her bed. Walking quietly for so big a man, he came around to stand beside her and began to speak softly, hoping to penetrate her semi-conscious state enough that she would know who was present when she awoke.

Her hair was fanned out across the pillow, and dark, tiny wisps had plastered her heart-shaped face in damp disarray. He resisted the urge to touch her and had to satisfy himself with a vocal approach instead. All the while he was talking, he was thinking of the joy he'd felt, when he realized there were no tubes or machines hooked to her fragile body, beeping her life signs for all who entered to hear. That had to mean she was not in any serious danger. All he could see in the way of obvious injuries were the bandages on her hands. They were hard to miss since she kept waving first one and then the other weakly in the air, continuing to fight the man who'd attacked her. The sight was finally more than King could bear. He spoke a bit louder, trying to penetrate her dream world.

It was the first time in nearly three years that he'd seen Jesse. They'd spoken off and on, but always by phone. Jesse kept him at a distance emotionally, and King was still at a loss as to why. One day everything had been normal, and the next thing he knew, she had taken a job and left the Double M Ranch. He hadn't been able to decipher his feelings then, and he was still unable to put his feelings for Jesse into words. She was just his Jesse, the kid who'd followed him all over the ranch and then turned to him in desolation when Andrew McCandless died. The friendship he'd felt for the young girl had deepened into a close relationship with the woman. But he hadn't had time to absorb the difference before Jesse left. There was still a big hole in his life that no one had been able to fill.

He started to touch her, anything to stop the horrible nightmare that was stuck on instant replay in her mind. But the decision was taken from his hands. She thrashed out wildly, bumping one of her bandaged hands on the guard rail. The pain penetrated her semiconscious state with a rude awakening.

Jesse moaned and blinked, trying to assimilate her surroundings and the unfamiliar smells that assaulted her senses. Her heart accelerated. She couldn't stifle the small scream that slipped from her lips as she saw the silhouette of a tall man standing beside her bed. It was only after she heard the familiar, husky voice that she allowed her heart to slow down to a sprint instead of the race in which it had been indulging.

Oh God! she thought. *He looks so big and gorgeous and worried.* And for the first time since her ordeal had begun, Jesse felt safe.

"King?" she whispered, afraid to believe her own eyes.

"Jess," he said softly, holding out his hand to let her make the initial contact. "Oh, Jesse Rose, what did he do to you honey?"

It was the old, familiar term of endearment that did it. Jesse hadn't been able to cry, but now she felt it coming from so deeply inside her, she was afraid she couldn't stop. No one ever called her Jesse Rose but King. No one else would dare.

King reached down and lowered the guard rail on one side of her bed.

"Will you let me hold you, Jess? I just need to feel for myself that you're all in one piece. You've scared Maggie and me out of years we couldn't spare, sweetheart."

The husky plea was unnecessary, because the moment the rail went down, Jesse was in his arms.

He gathered Jesse, bedclothes and all, in a gentle but fierce embrace, breathing a sigh of relief in the dark cloud of hair on her neck. He felt her tremble and heard her trying to swallow the misery that wanted out of her heart.

"Just let it go, Jesse Rose. I've got you now, honey. And, I swear to God, no one will ever hurt you like this again. Do you hear me? No one!"

King swung her up in his arms, cradling her like he would a child, and carried her to a big, stiff-backed chair by the window. He lowered himself carefully and swaddled Jesse in his lap like a baby.

She let herself absorb the essence of this man...her King. Once he'd been her world. And then... She stifled the thoughts and buried her head against his shirt front instead. She couldn't deal with old hurts. The new ones were too overwhelming. Sobs flowed into deep, racking gulps of misery, and the strong arms that cradled her kept her from flying apart.

"I was scared, so scared, King. I thought I was going to die!"

"I know, honey. I know. It's okay now, Jesse," he muttered as he rocked her gently in his arms. "Cry all you want. I won't let you go."

Jesse cupped her bandaged hands carefully against her chest and let the tears flow, relishing the utter and complete feeling of security that crept inside her heart. For the first time since her attack, Jesse believed she would survive. She wasn't alone now. King wouldn't let anyone hurt her again. She believed that as surely as she knew the sun would rise each day.

The guard outside the door heard Jesse's sobs and carefully peeked inside to assure himself that all was

well. The big man seemed to have everything under
control. It was obvious that the girl was glad to see
him. He nodded once at King's sharp look of distrust
toward the opening door, and then quietly pulled it
closed.

Chapter 2

Several hours later, Captain Shockey and another officer who doubled as a police artist came down the hall to Jesse's room. The guard saw them approaching and stood at attention.

"Anything new?" Shockey asked, as he started into Jesse LeBeau's room.

"That McCandless fellow you called got here just before noon. He's still inside."

Shockey grunted in surprise. He looked down at his watch and noted it was almost four in the afternoon. Almost twenty-four hours had elapsed since the girl's attack, and they still had no strong leads. Just a blood type, the knife the girl had taken away from the intruder, and a trail of blood that ended in the middle of a street. No fingerprints, no witnesses other than the girl, and she hadn't been able to give much of a description. Shockey was hoping the police artist could get more since she'd had a chance to calm down. Shockey was beginning to believe this wasn't just a random, spur-of-the-moment attack. It had been thought out to the degree that the perpetrator was wearing some kind of surgical gloves and had an accomplice waiting. But waiting for what? If they had been planning to steal her belongings, the accomplice had waited. It was too far to carry televisions, stereos, silver, and the like. And, in Shockey's experience, someone intent on rape or murder didn't usually work with an accomplice. Something just didn't ring true on this one. *Well,* he thought, as he stepped around the guard at the door, *maybe we'll get lucky and come up with a pretty good sketch.*

King was dozing between trying to balance himself in the stiff-backed chair and stretching his long legs against the corner wall while still cradling Jesse safely in his arms. She looked so tiny and so hurt, yet there was something different about her. He supposed it was just that he hadn't seen her in so long. He gazed hard at the delicate shape and plane of her face while he held her against his heartbeat. While he was trying to absorb this new and different person he held so intimately within his arms he fell asleep.

The sound of the door hitting against the back wall woke him instantly. He straightened up from his slumped position, knew he was going to have a crick in his neck, and glared silently at the intruders, indicating with a look at Jesse that they keep quiet. It did little good. Evidently the older of the two men who entered wasn't the patient type.

"You'd be King McCandless," he said, making no effort to lower his voice.

Jesse jumped at the sudden, loud voice and uttered a small cry of fright as she awakened to two men looming over her.

"Dammit!" King muttered. "It's okay, Jesse," he said roughly, and began to pull himself from his slumped position while not losing his hold on Jesse.

"What? What's wrong?" Jesse asked, trying to absorb the presence of the other men in her room. She sensed King's antagonism. Had something happened while she was asleep that she'd missed?

"Nothing's wrong, honey," King muttered. He laid Jesse back in bed, quickly pulling the covers around and over her to shield her bare legs and thighs from the two men. "They were just leaving."

Jesse recognized the ominous tone of voice and knew that, if she didn't intervene, King would find himself in trouble for assaulting a police officer.

"Wait, King," Jesse urged, placing a bandaged hand carefully on King's arm. It wasn't much of a restraint, but her voice was all that was necessary. King focused on the intensity of her eyes, imploring him to listen. "They're police. They told me earlier, before you arrived, that they would be back. I just forgot. Captain Shockey," Jesse said. "This is King McCandless. He's the son of the man who finished raising me after Daddy died. He's just about all the family I have.''

A funny pain shot through King's chest as Jesse spoke the words ''all the family.'' He hadn't realized how true that was, and felt guilty that he'd let so much time pass without forcing her to come home, or at least talk about what made her leave. Unfortunately, now was not the time. Jesse's imploring look slowed his anger and he gently brushed the hair away from her face. He sighed, then turned back to the men.

''Shockey,'' he acknowledged, as the older of the two men shook hands with him.

''Sorry for the intrusion,'' he said, for all who cared to listen. It was all the apology they would get. He had a job to do. ''This is Officer Ramirez, Miss LeBeau. He's going to try and help you remember all you can about the man who attacked you and then try to draw his likeness. But he'll need your help. You've got to think of the intruder, what he looked like, what he felt like, what he smelled like.'' He saw the look of horror on the woman's face and wondered if she had enough spunk in her to do the job. She'd been through a lot already. ''I know you don't want to, little lady. But I need you to close your eyes and pull this man out from wherever you've buried him. Okay?''

His blunt, matter-of-fact manner was just what Jesse needed to fortify herself for the ugly job ahead of her.

Jesse's lips trembled and the tears that pooled in her eyes slipped down her cheeks, past the dark, purple bruise on her face. King shook with fury. She wasn't up to this. He started to intervene when Jesse's voice stopped him.

"I'll do whatever it takes, Captain. I want him caught more than you do. If he's not, I'll never feel safe again."

"Good girl," he said, and motioned for Ramirez to come forward.

The police artist had been through this many times and did all he could to put the victim at ease. His low, soothing voice and casual manner soon had Jesse absorbed in trying to remember every minute detail.

As Jesse worked with the police artist, losing herself in the task of remembering what she'd been so desperately trying to forget, King stepped away from her bed and motioned Shockey aside.

"When they let Jesse go," King said, "I'm taking her back home with me." His words were almost a dare for the older man to disagree. To King's surprise, he did not.

"Probably a good idea. She doesn't need to be alone at this point." He squinted his eyes a bit as he leaned back and looked up at the big man who'd backed him into a corner of the room. Damned if he couldn't use someone like McCandless on the force.

"Where's home anyway?" Shockey asked, and pulled a notebook from his jacket pocket. "Might need more information from Miss LeBeau and you'll want to know when the man is apprehended. We'll need her to come back and identify him then, you know."

King nodded in agreement and the look of peace and

pleasure that suffused his face was noticeable when Shockey mentioned home.

"Home is the Double M Ranch southeast of Tulsa and Broken Arrow, Oklahoma. We raise a few cows, enough feed for them to get by, and once in a while, drill an oil well or two. But most of that was my father's love. Mine are the horses."

Shockey didn't raise an eyebrow, but he made a silent note to himself to do some more checking on this big man. *Drill an oil well or two,* he thought to himself with a grin. *Oilmen were a breed alone.* They were big gamblers, used to taking chances, but so were the horsebreeders.

"You race 'em?" he asked nonchalantly.

"No," King answered, and the light in his dark eyes gave away his deep love for the land and the horses that ran on it. "I raise them and sell them. And they're Arabians, not racehorses."

Arabians! That *was* a costly enterprise. Shockey knew he would certainly check into this man's background. He didn't know much about the business, but he suspected this man could probably buy or sell just about whatever he chose. There was an air about him. And that name...King. Hell of a name to stick on a man. He seemed to be doing okay with it, though. Didn't let it intimidate him at all. Shockey interrupted his own rambling thoughts and said, "Yeah, well, that's just about all I need here. When Ramirez is through, you're pretty much free to go."

"I'll need to go to Jesse's home before we leave to

get some of her things. Is there a problem with that?'' King asked, uncertain about disturbing a crime scene.

Shockey shook his head. ''Just let me know when you want to go and I'll meet you there. It's not pretty. You'll need to be prepared. I guess she'll want to clean it up before she moves. Not many people will stay in a home where something like that has happened to them. Not many can.''

King was taken aback. He hadn't even thought that far ahead. Shockey's words gave him something more to digest.

Shockey spoke briefly to Ramirez and frowned at the picture emerging on the flat white surface of artist's paper.

King watched Shockey leave and felt like he'd just been sized up and found lacking. He didn't think he would ever like him personally, but suspected Shockey was very good at his job.

Ramirez finally finished with a promise to let King have several copies of the sketch to take back home with him.

''I didn't remember much more,'' Jesse said morosely, fidgeting with the sheet covering her legs. ''It all happened so fast, I just didn't concentrate on what he looked like as much as getting the knife and getting away from him.''

''You did all you could, Jess,'' King said, watching her face for signs of stress. ''More than most.''

The ordeal had been very trying for her. She'd had to go over and over every phase of the attack while helping the artist, and more than once had broken down in tears at a particularly traumatic point. His heart ached for her.

She shrugged and sighed, slumping down into the muddled pile of bedcovers, and tried with little success to brush the hair away from her face and neck. There wasn't a lot one could do with both hands bandaged. Someone had to help her bathe, go to the bathroom, brush her teeth, eat. There was virtually nothing Jesse could do for herself at this point, and she was frustrated beyond belief.

King watched her for a moment and then offered a suggestion.

"Jesse, would you like me to brush your hair? I know the nurses help you all they can, but most of their grooming is hit and miss. I guess they're just too busy for more."

The offer was a welcome one. And, with a bit of twisting and rearranging, King was soon giving her tousled hair a new look.

The brush bit through her hair, digging through the tangles all the way to her scalp. It felt wonderful. King's husky voice and the long, soothing strokes relaxed Jesse as nothing else possibly could. She groaned aloud in pleasure and closed her eyes at the almost sensual feel of the deep, repetitive strokes.

"That feels absolutely wonderful," Jesse whispered, and opened her eyes to see King watching her in the small mirror opposite her bed. She couldn't tell what he was thinking, but he had a most interesting expression on his face. She smiled to herself as she thought, *He looks like he's just seen a ghost.* Then she decided, *Maybe he didn't see a ghost. Maybe he just saw a stranger.*

Jesse knew King was used to seeing her as the gangly twelve-year-old child, desolate in the face of her father's death, and then as a late-blooming teenager, self-conscious of a maturing figure, and with no one to explain life's mysteries except a very kindly housekeeper thrust in the role of mother. He had never seen her as Jesse LeBeau, the woman. It was about time.

King was dumbstruck. He'd accidentally caught a glimpse of Jesse's face in the mirror as he worked, and the sight of her eyes closed, her lips slightly parted in sensual delight as the brush bit into her scalp, her head tilted back, resting against his chest as he brushed, had made another, more intimate thought pop into his head. It startled him that he'd ever considered it. It made King realize he didn't even know this woman. He knew who she'd been. He just didn't know who she'd become. King couldn't get the idea out of his head that she would look exactly like that as someone made love to her. That thought followed with an instant flash that he didn't want anyone putting that look on her face but him. Guilt, shock, and a bit of intrigue flowed through him and his hands stilled, forgetting why he held the hairbrush, or why Jesse was propped up against him. He just stood and stared at her image in the mirror, unaware that Jesse was staring back.

Her slow, teasing drawl broke the silent staring match, and King's face flushed a dark red as she spoke.

"You're very good with your hands," she said, knowing that he was going to take it the wrong way. She'd seen the way he was looking at her. She also knew it was going to embarrass him and she delighted in the flush it produced.

"Uh, yeah. I guess so," he mumbled, trying to get off on a different subject. "I should be," he said. "I do most of the brood mares' grooming myself."

Jesse's eyebrows shot up, tickled beyond words that he'd just claimed his expertise with a brush lay entirely in his skill of horse grooming. Not the most recommending thing he could have said in reference to Jesse's hair. Her delight echoed in the room while King's face got redder and redder, as he realized what he'd just said.

"You little witch," he growled, knowing Jesse had been teasing him. He wasn't sure just how much he'd revealed of his thoughts, but she'd been sharp enough to pick up on some of them. He didn't care that she was laughing at his expense. The pleasure he got from hearing her laugh at all was worth it.

"Sorry," Jesse said, as she finally caught her breath between giggles. "But you were asking for it. Horses indeed!"

King smiled back, allowing her to enjoy that much of his faux pas. Thank God she hadn't picked up on the rest of it.

Little did he realize, but Jesse knew exactly, or so

nearly that it didn't matter, what he'd been thinking. She wasn't dreading going back to Oklahoma with him. Maybe it was finally time.

The blue van turned off the street into a narrow, tree-lined driveway leading to Lynch's place. The driver silently cursed the day he'd decided to let Lynch handle the kidnapping. It had been so simple. No one was to get hurt, everyone was going to get rich, and Jesse LeBeau would be turned safely loose later. King McCandless would be a less wealthy man, but that would have been okay with the driver. It wasn't fair how some people had so much money and others, like him, never had enough. To make matters worse, it had cost the driver a pretty penny to get Lynch patched up and not have it reported to the police.

The driver stopped in front of a small, run-down duplex partially hidden behind a row of oversized lilac bushes. The leaves on the bushes were limp and dusty, suffering in the July temperatures from lack of water and care, just like the whole area. The shabby surroundings fit the driver's idea of where Lynch would live. He looked in disgust at the house, and then back at the pitiful excuse for a man dozing in his passenger seat, slamming his fists against the steering wheel in frustration and shouting.

"Wake up, Sleeping Beauty! Get out of my sight and stay indoors until you're healed. Your stupid face, vague though the rendering may be, was plastered all over the news this evening. Even I recognized you. All you need to telegraph your part in this disaster is to venture outside plastered with bandages and stitches.''

Lynch stared, his doze disturbed by the driver's vehemence. He looked around in surprise, noted the familiar house, and for the first time in longer than he could remember, thought that he was glad to be here.

''I'll be in touch,'' the driver snarled. ''So don't get any ideas about leaving town. We're not through with each other just yet.''

Lynch nodded, opened the door, and very carefully lowered himself and his duffle bag from the van. He hurt in so many places, he couldn't have argued to save his soul. Besides, he knew he'd bungled enough already. The least he could do was keep his mouth shut. He knew this man well enough to know that his looks belied his true nature. He was very dangerous.

He watched the driver try to maneuver the van out of the narrow drive without the aid of a rearview mirror. He had to back out the same way he'd come in and wasn't doing a very good job. A small, wilting bunch of marigolds went under the wheels of the van and a piece of an overgrown hedge with it. He saw the driver's mouth moving at a very fast pace and knew he was probably cursing him and everything in sight. Therefore, he decided to remove himself from sight and lessen the number of things upon which the driver could vent his fury.

He entered the duplex, shutting himself away from the eyes of the world.

* * *

Maggie was putting the finishing touches to Jesse's old room, anxious to have her last chick back in the nest, if only for a while. She frowned as she heard the sounds of a car coming down the graveled driveway. She knew without looking that it was Duncan. He always drove too fast. He did everything fast. Even life was lived at fast-forward. Maggie personally thought that he missed the best life had to offer because he never took time to look for the little things. Maggie did her best to hide her disapproval of Andrew McCandless's younger brother. However, she suspected Duncan was all too aware of her opinions.

Duncan had only been ten when his beloved older brother, Andrew, became a father. From the first, he'd resented the child. King! The very name had burned a brand of hate in his heart. And then when Shirley, Andrew's wife, died less than a year later from a fall off a horse, King drew even more attention. Orphan indeed! What did they think he was? His parents had been dead so long he could barely remember what they looked like. Andrew was the only parent he acknowledged. Duncan fostered the antagonism and hate with a subversive skill. None, save possibly Maggie, knew just how deeply he resented being the McCandless that didn't count.

Maggie sighed loudly as she heard him enter the house with his usual lack of manners. He didn't live here anymore and as far as she was concerned, family or not, he should knock.

"Maggie? Anybody?" Duncan called, turning

around in the hallway, trying to locate some member
of the family. He saw himself in the hall mirror as he
turned, and lifted his hand to pat a lock of hair back
into place. The act was unconscious. He was good-
looking and knew it. Except for the ten years separating
them, he and King could have passed for twins.

Maggie came down the hallway in time to see Duncan's act of vanity. *That figures,* she thought, and then
answered Duncan before he could call out again.

"Here," she said, and found herself swinging about
the room, lifted off her feet in his exuberance.

"Where is everybody?" he said, as he twirled Maggie around and then planted a kiss on her cheek. He
put her back on firm ground with a tweek of her face.

"Stop it, you fool," Maggie spluttered, trying to pull
her dress and apron back into place. She didn't even
want to think how her hair must look. Its usually neat
bun was probably coming apart at the seams.

"Maggie, love, you like it and you know it," he
teased, and then repeated his question. "Where's King?
I need to talk to him."

Duncan watched an odd expression come and go in
the elderly housekeeper's eyes and knew something
was wrong.

"What?" he coaxed.

"King's not here," she said, and started toward the
back of the house to the kitchen, confident that he
would follow. He wouldn't leave until he got what he
came for and that was usually money. Also, Maggie
was more at home there, and she wanted to be on fa-

miliar territory when she broke the news about Jesse. Duncan wasn't going to take this well.

She suspected Duncan had always been attracted to Jesse, especially after she'd turned twenty-one. That's when she'd inherited the bulk of her father's estate that had been held in trust. There were shares in producing oil wells, a refinery, a goodly portion of the land of one of the newer Tulsa suburbs; the list went on and on. Michael LeBeau had not believed in banks. He'd invested nearly everything he made and, when he died, had been richer on paper than in the bank. Nevertheless, it had made Jesse a well-to-do woman. It just hadn't seemed to matter. She had continued her college studies and graduated from Tulsa University with a degree in education. It had delighted Andrew, but he didn't think for a minute that she would ever put it to use. He'd died believing Jesse's world would always be in order.

Maggie lifted a large bowl down from one of the cabinets and began to assemble the ingredients necessary for double fudge chocolate cake. It was Jesse's favorite.

"Maggie," Duncan persisted, "where *is* King, if he's not here?" He sighed to himself and resisted the urge to shout. She was so infuriating. She knew what he wanted. Why didn't she just come out and tell him? Everybody treated him like a fool. If they only knew, he was nobody's fool.

"We got a call. Jesse's been hurt. She's..." but she wasn't allowed to finish her sentence.

"Hurt?" he shouted. "Why wasn't I notified? What happened? Was it a car accident? What? Dammit, woman, talk. Don't I count for anything around here?" He grabbed Maggie roughly by the shoulders and shook her.

"You weren't notified because, as usual, you weren't home," Maggie said, and shrugged out of his tight grasp. "And…it wasn't an accident. Someone tried to kill her."

The look on Duncan's face surprised Maggie. Tears came to his eyes and his mouth worked, trying to speak past the emotion that threatened to choke him. He finally pulled himself together and wiped a hand roughly across his face. He reached blindly behind him and, when he felt the wooden back of the kitchen chair, lowered himself carefully into the seat as if his legs would no longer hold him.

"Kill her?" he mumbled. "No…no, not kill her. How bad is she hurt? Is she…disfigured in any way?"

Maggie gasped aloud at his lack of sensitivity and then frowned. That *would* matter most to someone of his caliber. She refused to answer him until he looked up with a pitiful expression on his face. She reluctantly relented.

"King called about two hours ago," she said, continuing to measure ingredients into the mixing bowl. She had to keep herself busy, too. She was too horrified by what had happened to her girl to let herself stop and think of the implications until she actually held Jesse in her hands. "I don't think she's hurt too badly. She had some severe lacerations on her hands and some bruising on her face, but other than that, I believe she's okay.''

"Thank God!'' he whispered aloud, and buried his face in his hands. "If her injuries are minimal, then we must be thankful that she is alive. I'm just so glad she's still the same.''

"I doubt she'll ever be the same,'' Maggie snapped, and began stirring vigorously. She had to do something to keep her hands off this man. He made her so mad.

Duncan got slowly to his feet and shoved his hands in his pockets. He began backing out of the kitchen, bidding Maggie goodbye as he continued his crawfish exit.

"I'll call you later to check on Jesse. Maybe I'll go see her as soon as she's able to go home.''

"She's not going home. King is bringing her here,'' Maggie said.

"Here? Wonderful,'' Duncan said, his attitude of dejection changing by the minute. "I'll just give them time to settle in, and then I'll be over. Cheer her up and all. It'll be great to see her again.''

"You better call first,'' Maggie warned, but her words bounced off the front door. Duncan McCandless was gone. He'd disappeared as quickly as he'd appeared.

She shook her head, dismissing the futility of trying to make him into something he was not. His brother Andrew had been the only one with any sense. King was following in his father's footsteps, but for some reason, Duncan McCandless just hadn't figured out how to grow up.

Chapter 3

King spent his nights with Jesse on a cot furnished by the nursing staff, going back to the hotel every day just to shower and change. He wanted to be at the hospital for her, as much for her protection as for her peace of mind. The intruder who'd attacked Jesse was still unapprehended. He'd simply vanished. The few leads the police received went nowhere. No hospital, no medical facility of any kind in the entire state, had reported a man with the kind of injuries Jesse had inflicted. The police had begun to talk of the possibility of the perpetrator lying dead and still undetected. However, neither King nor Captain Shockey agreed with that theory. They believed he was out there somewhere, hiding, biding his time.

King had been reluctant to leave Jesse for even a

short time until one of her friends from school heard of her attack. She started coming by every day after her summer classes were dismissed. Her name was Sheila. King liked her and could see why Jesse liked her, too. She was short and blond, funny and forthright, and best of all, she made Jesse smile. Everyone else skirted around Jesse's attack. They were afraid to say the wrong thing—afraid that what they said would hurt her feelings or bring back bad memories. But not Sheila. She was the best thing that could have happened at this point in Jesse's life. It did King good to hear Sheila's anecdotes and her suppositions of the probable nightmares Jesse's intruder was having, too. Sheila's nonsense was closer to the truth than they could have imagined. Lynch's days and nights were pure hell.

Lynch was going crazy. He'd been shut inside his house for days. The shades were drawn, and he had no way to cool himself in the sweltering heat. The utilities had been cut because of non-payment. He was running out of food. He needed to get some more peroxide to treat his slowly healing cuts and, most of all, he needed a drink. He'd made up his mind that, when it got dark, he was going out. There was an all-night convenience store less than four blocks from his duplex, and after midnight hardly anyone frequented the location. The only problem was that he didn't have any money. But he'd worry about that later. Right now, he needed a drink and he needed food. He settled back to wait for sundown. He had a plan.

* * *

King's phone call to Maggie had been just what she needed. He smiled as he replaced the receiver, patting his pockets to make certain he had all the papers and keys necessary to go back to the hospital. His assurance that Jesse was healing and that they would be home day after tomorrow was good news indeed. Her stitches were to come out in the morning. Then, after going over minor exercises in physical therapy, Jesse would be released.

But King still had to get inside Jesse's house and pack enough of her belongings for a long stay. He had made up his mind she wasn't coming back to St. Louis until it was safe. Now, he had to convince Jesse.

She wasn't going to be as easy to persuade as she'd been when he first arrived. Then, she'd been so frightened and in so much pain she'd pretty much let him make the rules. But as she grew stronger, so did her will. Jesse was obviously still very relieved to see King come back into her room each day, but she had re-erected that secret wall of silence between them. A couple of times King had tried to draw her out; get her to talk about her decision to leave the ranch. Each time, Jesse would change the subject. He knew in no uncertain terms that now was not the time. She wasn't ready to deal with it, so he let it drop. But time was running out, and so was King's patience. She *had* to come with him. She didn't have a choice until the intruder was caught.

The hospital room was dark and quiet. The only light

came from the hallway outside the partially opened door. King watched the play of emotions on Jesse's face. She hadn't said no. She hadn't said yes. In fact, she hadn't said anything at all. That was what was bothering him.

"Jesse, for the love of…" then he caught himself. Anger would get him nowhere. He took a deep breath and started over. "Honey, I just don't understand. The ranch is your home. You'll be safe there with your family."

But Jesse's soft interruption startled him. He didn't know what to make of it.

"I know that you'll take care of me, King. You always have. But you're not *really* my family. I don't have any family." The harshness of her words was softened with a smile. "Just very dear friends."

Her denial hurt in a way he could never have imagined, yet he refused to be deterred.

"Okay," he agreed, letting his breath out in slow, measured puffs of frustration. "I'm not your brother, but by God, I feel like one, and I want you safe. Is that so bad?"

He knew the instant he said he felt like her brother that he was lying to himself and to Jesse. But the thought behind it was sincere, and he let his statement stand.

Jesse read the hurt in his face and knew he'd never understand. That's partly why she'd left. She hadn't wanted a brother. She'd wanted more from King than he could give.

"I'm not your sister," she said more harshly than she intended, and took a deep breath before she continued. "Most of the time I don't feel like I belong to anyone. I teach other people's children, not my own. I go home to an empty house and grade papers until I get tired and, usually, I just go to bed. I know I made my choices, and though they aren't what I particularly desired, they're mine. But I appreciate, more than you can ever know, that you were here for me. I couldn't have survived this nightmare without you. And..."

King held his breath.

"And," she continued, "I'll come home with you. But just until the man is apprehended. Then I have to come back to this life and my job. This is my world now, King. It's the only one I belong to."

King breathed a huge sigh of relief and pulled Jesse into a big hug. He felt her momentary resistance and then smiled to himself as he felt her relax, allowing him the familiarity. Just as soon as he got her back to the ranch, he was going to get to the bottom of her silence.

Jesse knew every word she spoke and every denial she put in his way would only make King more determined to crack the shell of secrecy she'd erected around herself. She didn't know what was going to happen when she went back to the Double M with King. The only thing she did know was that pretending he was her brother was not going to work again.

Jesse was in therapy, being briefed on the types of exercises she must do to regain full mobility in her hands. Her stitches had been removed earlier in the day, and while she was horrified at the maze of tiny red lines crisscrossing her palms, she counted herself lucky to be alive still. Scars were something with which she could deal.

King had made arrangements with Sheila and Captain Shockey to meet at Jesse's house and pack the needed cloths for their trip. Sheila willingly agreed. She had been at Jesse's home often enough to be able to find anything they would need. Shockey had agreed earlier to accompany King. While it was still the scene of a crime, King had free access with Jesse's permission.

It was pure curiosity on Shockey's part to see how McCandless would react. He had a gut feeling there was more to Jesse LeBeau's attack than just a pervert crawling through a window. Until a case was solved, he trusted no one.

King's cab pulled into Jesse's driveway as Sheila and Shockey arrived. He was glad. He wanted to get this over with as soon as possible.

"It's not a pretty sight," Shockey warned as they entered the stuffy confines of the darkened interior.

Sheila shuddered and looked about nervously, half expecting someone to jump from behind a sofa or out of a closet.

"It wasn't a pretty thing to do to anyone. I don't imagine it is," King growled, his voice even deeper and rougher than usual. He raked his hand through his hair, ruffling the ends out of order. He just wanted this job over with. This was the first time he'd been to Jesse's home. He felt curious and a little guilty. He should have come sooner. He looked around, searching for signs of the Jesse he knew. There were none. It may as well have been a hotel room. Nothing looked lived in. There were no pictures, no mess, no personal items...nothing. Her life here was a puzzle. It looked like she'd just been eating and sleeping here, not really living. It almost looked like she'd been waiting. But waiting for what?

"Well, come on," King said. "Let's get this over with. Lead the way, Captain."

Shockey made a mental note. A plus for McCandless. He didn't know where the rooms were located. Funny, if they're so close, he hadn't been inside this house. Something didn't add up.

Sheila's gasp was nothing to the rage King felt as they walked into Jesse's bedroom. Nothing had been cleaned, nothing had been moved. For the first time he realized just how valiantly Jesse had struggled and how desperately she'd fought to survive. His voice came out in a dark, ugly threat and his entire body shook as he turned to Shockey and growled a warning.

"You better find him before I do."

Shockey nodded with a silent promise as well as a silent warning to King, and then left them to their task.

It was completed in haste and silence. No one spoke much until they were outside.

"Sheila," King said, watching the little blond get

into her car. "I'm sorry you had to go through this. But Jesse and I really appreciate your help. I probably wouldn't have packed any of the right stuff."

"I didn't go through anything," she answered. "Jesse is the one who's suffered. And as far as help, I didn't do so much. She would have done the same, and more, for me." She started her car and began to back from the short drive, then stopped and lowered her window. "Take good care of Jesse," she called. "She's a good friend. Please don't hurt her!"

King frowned as he watched her hesitant wave and then she disappeared around the curve. Why would she think I'd hurt Jesse? None of this made any sense at all.

Physical therapy was a nightmare. Jesse was extremely nervous. Everyone was a stranger. She could hardly concentrate on the therapist's instructions, for her furtive observation of the people that kept coming and going through the therapy room. The guard hadn't come with her to therapy; at least she hadn't seen him. She desperately wished King would hurry and get back. This was the first time she'd been alone since the attack. The staff went about daily duties and Jesse wished she was back in her room. Everytime she saw someone that fit the general description of the intruder, her heart would skip a beat. Twice she'd forced herself not to demand the unsuspecting men remove their shirts so she could see for herself if there were wounds on their upper bodies. She was driving herself into a state of paranoia she knew wasn't healthy. But someone she didn't know had tried to kill her. Until he was apprehended, Jesse was going to be afraid.

"Dear Lord," Jesse whispered to herself. "What if they never find him? How do I learn to cope with this?"

Finally the therapist was through. She left with a promise to tell a nurse that Jesse could go back to her room. Jesse sighed impatiently as she watched her exit between the tall, swinging doors that led back into the hall. It had been a matter of some argument whether she should walk down one floor to have her therapy. Finally, they had insisted she be brought down in a wheelchair. It was hospital policy. So she waited for someone to come and take her back to relative safety.

Jesse alternated between anticipation and joy when she thought about going back to the ranch with King—seeing Maggie again, all her old friends, and, she'd have to admit to herself, even Duncan.

Duncan! How could someone who looked so like King be the absolute and total opposite in personality? Duncan was the dark. King was the light. As a child, that was how Jesse had pictured them. But Duncan was a McCandless and she was not. Any problems she had with him were to be kept to herself. She was the outsider, not he. So she held her silence.

Her daydreams were interrupted as the swinging double doors opened. A man wearing hospital whites entered, pushing a wheel chair. Jesse's heart gave a sharp thud and she began to shake. He looked like...he was the same age and build. Jesse looked around wildly. He couldn't be coming for her. It had to be for someone else. It was then she realized she was all alone in the room. The man kept coming toward her with a smile on his face. She stood, frantically searching for an exit, a door into another room. Somewhere to run. A place to escape? There was nothing!

"Miss LeBeau?" the male nurse questioned, as he saw her agitation escalate. Something was wrong. Maybe they'd sent him to the wrong place. Or maybe this wasn't the right patient. "I came to get you and…" but he never got to finish his sentence.

"Nooo!" Jesse moaned softly, and started backing slowly away. Her fear was so great she didn't think she was going to be able to breathe. She couldn't go through this again. He said he came to get her. She was too frightened and hurt to fight again. "Please," she begged, holding her hands out in front of her with a motion for him to come no closer. *Oh God! Not again!*

Suddenly it dawned on the man. He knew who this was and he wanted to wring his supervisor's neck. This was the young woman who had been attacked several days ago. They should have known to send a female nurse. They'd made such a point of having no men enter her room, and this mistake, innocent though it may be, could do her irreparable harm. It was obvious to him that he was a vivid reminder of her recent ordeal.

"Miss LeBeau, please." He spoke in a calm, authoritative manner. "I'm not going to hurt you. I'm just a nurse. But I understand, okay? You wait there and I'll call someone else to take you back to your room.''

Jesse knew he was talking. She could see his lips moving. But the blood was roaring in her ears so loudly, she couldn't hear what he was saying. Then he stopped. He was backing slowly toward the door. She saw him call out to someone in the hall. She stood helplessly, waiting in terror.

"I need some help down here," he called urgently, motioning toward the nurses' station. "Some of you get down here quick, and you better be female."

King and one of the staff doctors were on their way to physical therapy to see how Jesse was progressing. He wanted to talk to the therapist himself and see if there was anything specific he might do to help her regain mobility in her fingers and hands after they went back to the ranch.

He saw a male nurse standing at the end of the long hallway, half in and half out of the swinging doors, saw a flurry of activity at the station as several of the nurses started hurrying toward the man in the doorway, and felt a twinge of apprehension. When he got close enough to read the sign over the doorway where they were headed, he started to run. It was the physical therapy room. Something was wrong and instinct told him it was with Jesse.

King heard the male nurse's low voice explaining the situation as the others arrived. His suspicion was confirmed. He looked past the group standing bunched in the doorway as they discussed the best possible way to handle the situation without further endangering the patient. King started to push past them.

"You can't go in there, mister," a nurse said. "There's a patient in there who needs special help. The staff psychiatrist is on his way."

"She doesn't need anything but me," King growled, and started to force his way through the group. "What in hell did you people do to cause this?" he muttered. "She was fine when I left."

"Let him pass," the doctor said as he arrived, quickly assessing the situation.

King stepped inside the door and looked around, trying to determine what had triggered this reaction. He could see nothing obvious but Jesse's intense fear. How was he going to get through to her without causing her harm? He waited, hoping she would come to him. But she didn't move, and the expression of horror on her face didn't change.

Jesse had backed herself as far into the room as she could go. When she felt the corner of the wall cradle her back, she slid down weakly into a crouched position, unable to run any farther. She hadn't taken her eyes from the man standing in the doorway.

The man was talking to people on the other side of the door, but she couldn't see their faces. Maybe he called for help. If there were too many, she couldn't fight them all. She moaned softly and beat her fists weakly against her knees. Jesse's rationale was gone. She had flashbacked to the original attack, and was living it all over again.

Her breath came in sobs as she frantically searched the room's sparse furnishings for some kind of weapon. She'd had one before, but she couldn't seem to find it now when she needed it. The man was going to kill her. She just knew it! Her eyes followed the baseboard as it ran the length of the room, still searching. There! Under the window! A piece of pipe! That would work! Jesse fixed on the pipe's location and began crawling on her hands and knees, oblivious to the pain in her palms as she pulled herself across the floor. Someone was coming through the doorway. She had to hurry. Jesse was breathing in harsh, choking gasps, her mind fixed on gaining control of the weapon. She still wasn't ready to die. Her fingers closed around the piece of metal as she clutched it tightly with both hands. She pulled herself upright and stood silhouetted against the backdrop of the bright midday sun streaming through the windows.

"Oh, dear Lord!" one of the nurses whispered to herself, as the group stood in shock, witnessing the terror and strength of heart that Jesse LeBeau possessed. Tears burned and blurred the nurse's vision as she turned away, unwilling to witness the suffering caused by the rape of Jesse LeBeau's mind.

"Be careful," the doctor urged as King entered, standing ready to assist if physical restraints became necessary. He was surprised that this had happened. The patient had seemed in control. He supposed that alone should have alerted him. No one could experience this type of trauma and not suffer some kind of emotional stress.

"Jesse," King called. He stood unmoving in the center of the room. "Jesse, it's me, King. Honey, put the pipe down. You know I wont hurt you, don't you, baby?" He kept repeating the plea, over and over, hoping to reach some part of Jesse that was still rational.

The deep, husky rasp was so familiar. Jesse blinked furiously, trying to clear away the veil of tears that kept blurring her vision. She heard him calling, over and over, repeating her name in the same, safe, familiar voice. The man who'd hurt her hadn't said her name. He'd only screamed ugly, foul things. This man was different. He wasn't trying to hurt her. He wasn't screaming at her. Maybe… She began to lower the pipe.

King cursed softly under his breath and resisted the urge to wipe the sweat from his eyes. Any sudden movement could startle her and send her back into the nightmare.

"Jesse Rose," he called softly, and saw her begin to tremble. He breathed a harsh sigh of relief as he watched the pipe slip from her shaky fingers and bounce once before it rolled back against the wall.

"King?" Jesse whispered, suddenly aware of her surroundings. It was the strangest sensation. She didn't know how she came to be standing so far away from the door, nor why everyone was looking at her so curiously. Her hands hurt. They hadn't hurt like this in days. She gasped as she looked down at the rawness.

A few tiny drops of blood were seeping from one of the deeper scars.

"What happened?" she moaned, and stumbled, but didn't fall. King's strong, familiar arms gathered her close, pulling her safely against the comforting beat of his heart. She buried her face in the soft linen shirt, recognizing the aftershave and the low growl in his voice, and relaxed.

King caught her just as her legs gave way. He swung her up into his arms, softly murmuring over and over against her cheek.

Jesse clung to his strength. She felt as if she'd just run five miles uphill. She was limp and shaking, and more and more aware of the small group of people whispering among themselves as they witnessed the drama that had unfolded before their eyes.

"I'm sorry," she mumbled, slowly realizing what must have happened, and embarrassed at the turmoil she'd caused. She turned her tear-stained face up to King, searching his face for approval. All she saw was a hard, tight-lipped expression and flat, angry fury in his eyes. She thought it was directed at her. "I got scared," she began. "And I couldn't find the guard, and you weren't here..."

"No!" King said, brushing a gentle kiss against her brow. "Don't you apologize for anything, Jess." His dark eyes flashed as he continued. "We're the ones who should be sorry. I shouldn't have left you, and—" his voice held a definite promise of menace

"—I don't know where in hell your guard is, but I'll bet I find out."

Jesse knew that tone of voice and the expression on his face. She'd never been the recipient of his anger, but she'd been a witness. It wasn't pretty.

"King," she cautioned, trying to pull herself together enough to think. "You can't do this." Her tone was that of a mother to a child, and oddly enough, King paused to listen. "You can't take the guard out behind Tilley's Bar and Grill. We're not back home in Tulsa. You can't hurt the officer."

"No," he muttered, "but I can damn sure hurt his feelings. And when I find him, I will."

Jesse sighed and leaned her head under his chin. She'd give him the right to that much. She wondered where the damn guard was, too.

Suddenly she was overwhelmed with the need to be through with all this. She was so ready to leave the hospital, St. Louis, and the whole terrible nightmare behind. She wanted to go home.

Sundown came, and with nightfall also came relief from the sweltering heat. Up went the shades and windows, and whatever breeze was strong enough to penetrate the dense shrubbery around the shabby duplex was welcomed. Lynch sat in the darkness by an open window and listened to the sounds of the neighborhood, as one by one, voices quieted and lights went out in the surrounding houses. Finally, all that disturbed the night was the occasional frenzied barking of a dog that was quickly silenced by its owner's angry shout.

It was time. Lynch wasn't waiting any longer. He needed out and he needed a drink. He had searched the unkempt closets all afternoon for something to wear that would cover his wounds and still not look out of place in the extreme heat. He'd come up with some old jean shorts and a T-shirt with a high neck and three-quarter length sleeves. It was the best he could do. His rummaging had solved another problem. He didn't have any money, but he'd found a partially used pad of blank checks from his lucrative days as a working man.

He felt a burning anger inside at the unexpected turn his life had taken. He wouldn't be in this miserable shape if it weren't for that woman. She'd messed up everything. He would have been fixed for life if she'd just cooperated. Instead, here he was, broke and injured, and it was all her fault. Then his anger turned toward the man who'd drawn him into this ill-fated scheme. Some big wheel he'd turned out to be. He hadn't even paid him for his trouble, and he hadn't come back like he'd promised.

Lynch patted his pocket, assuring himself that the checks were in place. He had no remorse about writing a check on a closed account. He planned to be long gone before the check had a chance to bounce.

Damn, but it feels good to be outside, Lynch thought as he pulled the front door shut behind him. He stood in the shadows, glancing furtively around to make certain he was unseen. Satisfied that he was unobserved, he started down the narrow drive with an almost jaunty air.

He stood underneath the eaves behind the convenience store and waited for the lone customer to pay for his gas and leave. The fewer people who saw him, the better off he would be. Finally the customer left. Lynch hesitated no longer.

"How ya' doin'?" he asked the clerk, as he sauntered in and pulled a scrap of paper from his pocket. "Just need a few things," he volunteered unnecessarily, and started searching the aisles.

Carefully noting the customer was alone and on foot, the clerk nodded and continued to refill a cigarette rack over the cash register. It didn't pay to be careless in a job like his and he didn't like working this shift anyway.

"This'll do it," Lynch said, as he carried the last of the items—two six-packs of beer—to the counter.

The clerk nodded and began ringing up the items. He rang up the total, told Lynch the amount owed, and began to sack the small pile of foodstuffs.

Lynch casually wrote out the check for the amount of purchase only, just as the sign at the cash register requested. Then he slid the check and his I.D. to the clerk.

The clerk was tired, distracted by the fact that he was having to work this graveyard shift, and anxious to get the lone man from his store. He took the check without even asking for a second identification and stuffed it into the cash drawer.

His "thank you, come again," was muttered as an afterthought.

Lynch was jubilant. He'd done it. He grabbed the sacks, one in each hand, and used his chest and stomach as props for the cumbersome load. But he couldn't mask his pain as one of the heavier sacks pressed sharply against his healing cuts.

"Hey, buddy," the clerk asked, as he saw the grimace on the man's face. "You all right? Need any help?"

"Naw," Lynch mumbled, biting his lip to keep from swearing as beads of sweat popped out on his forehead. "No problem. I'm just a little sore. Had an accident a while back and I ain't quite healed."

The clerk nodded, continuing to watch as Lynch juggled the sacks to a better, less painful position. Finally, satisfied that he could manage the load, he backed away from the counter and started out the door.

"Hey, mister," the clerk yelled sharply, "you're bleeding."

Lynch cursed under his breath and continued walking out the door. The heavy sacks had re-injured a slow-healing cut. Hurrying more with each step he took, he refused to acknowledge the clerk's observation. He didn't look back.

The clerk watched the man disappear into the darkness. Then something made him go to the door, just to see which way the man went. But he'd hesitated a bit too long. No matter how hard he looked, he saw nothing beyond the ring of light shining down on the store parking lot. He had started back inside when a police notice taped at eye level by the door caught his attention.

It was a sketch of a man wanted in connection with the attack on a woman in St. Louis. As he read, he remembered seeing something about it on the news, but he'd heard no more and had forgotten all about it until he began to read the notice. He chuckled to himself, remembering as he read that the woman had turned the tables quite nicely on this creep. He looked at the picture again. Something…something about the shape of the nose and mouth looked familiar. He remembered reading that the man would have suffered multiple stab wounds on his upper body. His heart jumped, and then raced. *What if…?* He cursed, absorbing what he'd just read and then looked back out into the night.

"Hell," he muttered, "let it go. Who wants to get involved with the cops?" But he couldn't get the woman out of his mind.

He went back to stocking the shelves along the narrow aisles, trying to put the incident and growing suspicions out of his mind. But his conscience wouldn't allow it, and with a snort of disgust, he went to the phone and dialed the number printed on the police sketch. It probably wouldn't amount to anything, but he'd never be satisfied until he made the call.

The call from the convenience store clerk was the

first solid lead the St. Louis police department had received. Shockey took the follow-up interview himself.

He listened intently to the clerk's recitation of events leading up to the blood appearing on the man's shirt, took note of the type of clothing he'd worn and the odd, almost furtive manner in which he'd left the store.

"Was he in here long?" Shockey asked.

"No, he didn't have over half a dozen items. If it hadn't been for the six-packs of beer, it'd all have fit into one sack, easy."

"Do you happen to remember what he bought?" Shockey asked, and turned the end of his Eversharp, adjusting the new lead to just the right length.

"Oh, I dunno," the clerk muttered. "You know, the usual junk food. This stuff ain't exactly supermarket quality. Uh...let me see. There was bread, a stick of that summer sausage, some cans of vienna sausage, the beer of course...and, oh yeah!" he added. "A package of Oreo cookies. I think that's about all." Then he remembered. "No, wait! I forgot about the other stuff. But it wasn't nothing to eat. He got a bottle of peroxide and some of them big patch adhesive bandages." He looked pleased with himself as he recalled the events. This was just like on TV.

Shockey made note of the last two items and suppressed a surge of elation. It was too soon to assume this was his man. But, so far, so good. Shockey was not one to jump to conclusions.

"So," Shockey repeated. "He paid you, took his stuff and left. Is that about it? He didn't happen to mention where he lived, or worked...anything like that?''

"Naw. It was just like I said. I took his check. He took his food and walked out the door.''

Shockey absorbed what the clerk had said.

"He paid by check?" He couldn't disguise the surprise and elation in his voice. This guy couldn't be the one. Surely he wasn't that stupid. "Did he have identification?"

"Yeah, a driver's license," the clerk mumbled. "I didn't ask for more. Here's the check, though. Thought you might want to take a look at it. I almost forgot to tell you.''

Shockey took the check, made a note of the information he needed, and handed a copy of the info to one of his detectives. "Here, check this out right away. I want to know if this guy's on the up and up, and if his is a current address. And,'' he added, "I don't have to tell you to hurry, do I?''

"No, sir,'' came the answer, as the detective immediately disappeared.

Shockey turned his attention back to the clerk, who was obviously growing weary of the repetitive questions.

"You sure this is all you remember?''

"Yeah,'' the clerk sighed. "That's just about it. Like I said, I almost didn't call. He didn't look exactly like the sketch, but I didn't think I needed to remember what he looked like. He was just another customer.''

But Shockey knew there was one vital piece of evidence still left to recover. "I'll need to confiscate your surveillance tapes," he said.

The clerk looked blank and then understanding dawned as he looked up at the cameras above the cash register.

"The tapes!" the clerk cried, excited that there was still more he could contribute. "He'll be on the tapes."

This couldn't be the man, Shockey thought to himself, as he carried the tapes to his car. Surely no one was so stupid that they would commit a crime like attempted murder, then pay for something by check and get videoed all at the same time. Shockey almost laughed aloud. He couldn't be this lucky.

Chapter 4

King muttered an odd litany of gentle oaths as he heard the pilot's announcement that they would be landing at Tulsa airport in less than five minutes.

"Thank God!" Jesse heard him say, and couldn't resist a smile. She knew how King hated to fly and how valiantly he'd tried to mask his fear just to be strong for her. He was always in control of every situation; so dependable and reliable. This one weakness he tried to ignore was really quite endearing.

King's solution to things over which he had no control was to ignore them. Unfortunately, it was very hard to ignore the fact that he was thousands of feet above the ground.

Jesse's stomach did a flip-flop of its own as the plane touched down on Oklahoma soil. In spite of all her protests and hesitation, she was very glad she'd decided to come with King. She knew that if she was ever to get over the intense terror she felt when she was alone, and the paranoia she had experienced in the hospital therapy room, it would be here, with those who loved her best.

King's fingers cupped her hand as the plane touched down, and she heard him sigh loudly in relief. Suddenly she was as anxious as King to get off the plane. She couldn't wait to set foot on McCandless territory. She hustled King from the plane, and aided in locating their luggage. It was only after they'd loaded the bags into the black Lincoln King retrieved from the parking garage that she felt she was finally on her way home.

"Thank you," Jesse whispered to King, then leaned over and softly pressed the firm cut of his cheek with her lips.

Her actions startled him. He was so intent on negotiating the ever-present detours on the downtown expressway that he nearly swerved into a large, orange barrel with a single flashing light.

"Hellfire," he muttered, as he quickly righted his course and looked about to see how many drivers behind and beside him were cursing his existence. "What was that for, girl?"

His heart had skipped at least two beats and was now doing overtime, trying to compensate. He didn't know why the simple act had so upset him. Jesse had kissed him plenty of times during her years at the Double M. But somehow this felt different. He angrily squashed

the thoughts that swiftly entered his mind. This was no
time to let his fancy wander. This was Jesse. He didn't
think of her like that...did he?

"Oh," Jesse sighed, her eyes dancing with delight.
"It was for coming to get me. For bringing me home.
For just being you."

King smiled. He, too, was glad she was home. She'd
talked all during the flight about seeing Maggie, her
old friends on the ranch, and schoolmates. She'd deli-
cately *not* asked much about his confrontation with the
negligent hospital guard. Jesse had talked about every
thing and everybody except Duncan. King wondered
why he was so conspicuously omitted. But before he
had a chance to ask, Jesse's excitement distracted his
line of thought and it was forgotten in the delight he
felt as she turned in the seat beside him.

"We're here," she announced, pointing to the two
giant oak trees that stood sentinel at the gate of the
Double M Ranch.

Jesse's eyes were shining, a mirror reflection of the
clear, blue brightness of the Oklahoma sky. She let
herself absorb the healing power of home—the soft,
rolling hills that flattened out into wide valleys, fenced
off from the long, graveled road snaking between the
scattered stands of native trees—home! Everything was
so dry, wilted, and dust-coated. And Jesse thought
she'd never seen anything as beautiful. Although they
rode in air-conditioned comfort, it was obvious by
looking out of the window, that this was just a stop-
gap from the sweltering heat. They needed rain.

Oklahoma always needed rain this time of year. And, one day soon it would rain, and rain too much. Then they would have to cope with floods. That was Oklahoma. That was home.

The ranch and outbuildings came into view as they rounded the last sharp curve and the stand of post oaks. The many barns, sheds, granaries, and corrals where King's horses reigned supreme were in tip-top condition. The newly painted stalls housing the Arabian brood mares gleamed painfully bright against the landscape of quickly dehydrating vegetation. Jesse absently noted the height of prairie grass behind the horse barns and knew the early spring rains had sparked quick growth that was now close to being ready for harvest. Soon they would cut and bale the natural prairie grasses for highly prized horse fodder.

The main house came into view as they passed the first of the sheds where some of the farm machinery was stored. Jesse couldn't suppress the quickening tears. It was so dear and familiar. She'd spent the better part of her life growing up inside those walls. Nothing looked different. It was still a long, rambling structure that had been added to only once, when Maggie came to live.

Andrew McCandless had been in dire need of someone to oversee King's teenage years and then later, just when Maggie thought raising children was behind her, Jesse had arrived.

The house was cedar and brick with a verandah that ran the entire length of its front. It had not been landscaped professionally, but the shrubbery around the house was varied and healthy. Someone had been watering vigorously to keep it all looking so green. The lawns had not suffered, and the trees and shrubs looked well cared for. Jesse suspected Maggie had left all that to Wil Turner, the foreman. He had a real affinity for growing things and made no bones about his expertise.

"There's Maggie!" Jesse cried, and then choked back a sob. It was obvious she had been expected. Several more people had gathered on the verandah, waiting to see for themselves that their little Jesse was truly okay. "And I see Charlie…and Turner…and Harvey and…oh, King," she whispered thickly, trying not to cry.

He'd barely stopped the car before Jesse was excavated from the Lincoln's cool depths and swallowed by the crowd of well-wishers. She was quickly hustled into the house away from the heat, leaving King to deal with the luggage alone. He didn't care. He would have carried suitcases for a month just to have her back.

King placed the last of Jesse's bags on her bed so she would be able to unpack. Her hands were still quite tender and she wouldn't have been able to lift them. He hoped Sheila hadn't left out anything important. From the weight of the bags, he doubted it.

King smiled as he looked around the room. There were flowers on the dresser, on the bedside table, even on the window seat. Maggie had possibly overdone it a bit. Yet he knew how dear Jesse was to them all and suspected Maggie had sorely missed her presence over the last three years.

Jesse LeBeau had been the only female, other than Maggie, on the McCandless's domain for as long as King could remember. She reigned supreme and it was obvious from the welcome she'd just received that she still held the crown.

King looked around, satisfied that all was in order, then closed the door to her room. He followed the sound of voices coming from the kitchen and hurried to join the crowd.

Everyone was talking at once. King could hear the melee from the hallway and hoped it wasn't too much for Jesse. He needn't have worried. Wil Turner, long-time foreman of the Double M, had Jesse in a seat of honor. She'd always been a small child, and to keep her safe and out from under foot, whoever had been looking after her would usually seat her on a corral rail or the back of a pickup truck. Today it was the corner of the kitchen cabinet. Jesse was smiling, enjoying their banter, and allowing their high praise of her actions to heal her wounded spirit. Their praise would probably have angered severe feminists. But as far as they were concerned, it was the highest honor they could bestow. They vowed their Jesse had "fought like a man." She was a true heroine.

King remained unseen in the shadows of the kitchen doorway and allowed himself the luxury of watching Jesse. Her hair was dark and windblown, caressing her bare shoulders with a careless touch. The pink thing she wore was something between a dress and pants. King didn't know the name for the culotte-skirted dress, but he knew he liked it. It was soft and clung in all the right places to very feminine curves. Her long, bare legs dangled with carefree abandon. And, somewhere between the front door and the kitchen, Jesse had stepped out of her sandals. King smiled. She was truly home.

"Just look at that," Turner urged. The men gathered closer as he held Jesse's injured hands palm side up. "You got sand, little girl," he said gruffly, and patted her knee. "We're real proud of you, Jesse. And your daddy would have been, too. You've got real fightin' spirit. If I could just get my hands on..."

Jesse threw her arms around Turner's neck and kissed him soundly, stopping the threat from being spoken. Then she jumped down from the cabinet and gave each of her old friends the same blessing as they began to leave.

King wondered if he'd looked as dazed and silly when Jesse had kissed him.

"Come on, boys," Turner called, catching a glimpse of King's shadow in the doorway. "Time to get back to work." He turned and waved as they filed out the door. "Welcome home, girl. Don't you worry none. We'll take good care of you here."

Jesse felt like she'd been pulled through a "dust devil," one of Oklahoma's famous little whirlwinds that skips across prairies, sucking loose bits of sand

and grass up into its tiny vortex. She was hot, breathless, and as satisfied as she'd been in ages.

Jesse turned and faced the elderly housekeeper who'd remained oddly silent through most of the boisterous welcome. Tears rose, filling her eyes and blurring Maggie's image. But Jesse couldn't stop the flow. She didn't have to pretend with Maggie. She knew it all.

"Come here, love," Maggie crooned, and gathered Jesse into her arms. "It'll be all right. Time will heal everything he did to you. It will heal these," she gently patted Jesse's hands, "as well as what's inside." She pointed to Jesse's breast. "Now, if you think you can stand it, I just happened to have a big, double, chocolate fudge cake that's going begging. Don't suppose you want to ruin your dinner?"

Laughter bubbled from deep within Jesse's heart and pushed the fear and misery back where it belonged. It did her good to hear the threat Maggie had thrown in their faces over the years. Maggie had a tendency to bake the most mouth-watering treats in the county and then tell all who entered her kitchen that they couldn't have any for fear of spoiling their meal.

"How about my dinner?" King teased, as he entered the room.

"Nothing ruins your appetite," Maggie growled in a teasing fashion. "You may as well sit down, too. But don't think I'm always going to be this easy. This is a special occasion. We've got our girl back home, safe and sound."

Jesse smiled lovingly at Maggie's attempt to lighten the emotionally charged atmosphere and then flashed a conspiratorial look at King. It was all the prompting he needed.

Maggie rarely broke a rule and, adults or not, King and Jesse delighted in being recipients of the exception.

Jesse sighed, replete from the ice cold milk and rich chocolate treat. It was good to be home.

"Duncan called," Maggie told Jesse, as she and King helped clear away the dinner dishes.

King had been furtively watching Jesse's progress as she carefully scraped and stacked, doing everything except actually carrying dishes to the sink. He knew she needed to feel useful, but didn't want her to overdo things on her first day.

The look that passed through Jesse's eyes, clouding their brightness, when Duncan's name was mentioned surprised him. It was something between revulsion and fear. Jesse's silence spoke loudly to his instincts. He wondered, as he continued to carry plates and bowls to the sink, what else was going on with Jesse that he knew nothing about.

Maggie's prattle fell into the silence, using up the emptiness in the kitchen. She seemed to be the only one unaware of her announcement's impact.

"He stopped by a couple of days after King left for St. Louis," she continued. "Seemed real upset at your news, Jesse." Then Maggie looked up. Her words ended abruptly. She sensed something was out of the ordinary, but didn't know what it was. She shrugged and finished her message.

"Anyway, he said he'd stop by tomorrow. I think he's a bit partial to you, Jesse," Maggie announced, and then couldn't resist rolling her eyes a bit at the unlikely thought. "About the only person besides himself he cares for." Realizing what she'd just said in King's presence, she blushed, but refused to refute the truth of her words.

King grinned wryly at Maggie, excusing her blunt statement as he'd always done. Maggie was as much family as anybody on the Double M and she had a right to her opinions. Unfortunately, this one was definitely on the mark. Duncan was a hard one to know.

The odd thing was that King had always been aware of Duncan's almost flirtatious manner around Jesse. It had never bothered him before. Duncan flirted with every woman within seeing distance...even Maggie. But this time Maggie's words hit King in a different way. He didn't think he liked the idea of Duncan and Jesse at all. From the expression on Jesse's face, neither did she.

"I told him not to come early," Maggie added, "but you know Duncan."

"That's fine," Jesse finally managed to say, aware King had noticed her hesitance. "I knew I'd see him sooner or later."

King frowned. It was such an odd acknowledgment of the impending visit. It seemed to him that she viewed it as something to get over with.

"If you two will excuse me," Jesse said, looking everywhere but at King. "I think I'll turn in early. It's been a long day."

"Sure," Maggie urged, bustling about the kitchen. "Go on to your room, honey. I'll be there shortly and help you get ready for bed."

"I think I'll be fine," Jesse said, and then caught herself before she refused all offers of help. There was one thing her hands still weren't strong enough to tackle. The faucets on the bathtub in her room were old and stiff. She knew she'd never get the water on.

"There's just one thing I may need help with and King can do that, dear," she said. Maggie looked worn to a frazzle. It had been a long day for someone her age as well. "You know how stiff the faucets are on my bathtub. I'll need someone to run my bath. Maybe in a day or two, when my hands get stronger, I won't have to ask."

"Sure I can, Jesse." King had also noticed how exhausted Maggie seemed to be. They were all so used to her coping with every aspect of ranch life that they hadn't noticed she was growing older. It was good that Jesse was back. Maggie needed company. "You go on to bed, too, Maggie. I'll lock up and see to Jesse's needs. After all, I haven't done such a bad job for the last few days, have I, Jess?"

Jesse smiled shyly and turned away, suddenly afraid he would see more in her expression than she wanted him to.

Maggie didn't argue. She just gave Jesse a weary

hug before heading toward her own rooms off the kitchen area. "Sleep tight," she called back, and then closed her door.

"Come on, Jesse Rose," King teased. "You're next. By the time I get all my women put to bed, it'll be time to get up."

All his women indeed! Jesse glared at his back as they walked down the hallway leading to the bedroom wing and wrinkled her nose at him in teasing fashion, knowing full well he couldn't see her actions.

"Just because you have no middle name," she muttered, "doesn't mean you need to wear mine out."

"Well," King answered, stating his point with unequivocal assurance. "After naming a baby King, what in hell else could follow?"

Jesse grinned and followed him into her room. She watched him disappear into her bathroom, and heard the sounds of water splashing full force into the depths of the old-fashioned claw-foot tub. She loved it, and had refused offers of having a new model installed years ago. It was long and deep, and was ideal for soaking. But the fixtures were old and stiff and resisted all but the firmest of grips.

"It's running," King announced, as he entered the bedroom area. "Need any help unpacking? I don't know what Sheila included, but if you don't have something you need, just make a list. I'll take you to Tulsa anytime you want to go."

"I'm sure I can manage," Jesse said, and continued to search through the open bags while King waited for the tub to fill. Her hands felt the familiar, well-worn softness. She smiled, pulling a faded, black, oversized T-shirt from beneath the neatly folded lingerie. Thank goodness for Sheila! She remembered.

"It's my favorite," Jesse said gleefully, holding it up under her chin and spinning around to the mirror over her dresser.

King watched the look of glee on Jesse's face and then saw what had made it appear. He didn't know whether to laugh or taste the smile on her face. The feeling that pulled at him was unfamiliar and probably marked the beginning of a sleepless night. He couldn't get past the image that flashed in his mind of taking that damn "Bo Knows" T-shirt off her body and making sure he was the only one who "knew" Jesse LeBeau.

"The tub's running over," Jesse cried, and dashed toward the bathroom, right behind King.

"Sorry," he mumbled, mopping at the floor with the fluffy white towels Maggie had provided. She was going to kill him for using them on the floor, but he'd grabbed them before he thought. "I'll get you fresh towels," he offered, then grinned sheepishly at the look of merriment on Jesse's face. "If you don't tell Maggie."

They both burst out laughing and the tenseness he'd felt moments earlier disappeared. He didn't know what was getting into him. Jesse didn't deserve his betrayal at this crucial time in her life, and he had no intention of frightening her with any sort of out-of-character behavior. She'd suffered all the surprises she needed for the time being.

"I'll be fine now," she said, pushing him out of the door of her room. "And, King," she called as he entered the door of his room across the hall, "thanks for everything."

She closed the door without waiting for an answer and King felt oddly alone.

Jesse had dawdled long enough. She'd unpacked, admired the flowers, taken a long, soaking bath, done the prescribed exercises on her hands, brushed haphazardly at her hair, and knew it was time. She was going to have to get in bed, turn out the lamp, and try to sleep. Just the thought of closing her eyes made her sick. She rubbed sweaty palms down the sides of her "Bo Knows" T-shirt and silently cursed the helpless feeling that was threatening to overwhelm her. Logically she knew she was safe. King was just across the hall. No one could hurt her here. But logic was lost in the terror that took over her senses when the lights went out and she was in bed...alone.

"Damn him," Jesse muttered aloud. "I won't let what that creep did—or tried to do to me—ruin the rest of my life. I won't."

She walked around the familiar old four-poster bed, pulled back the lightweight coverlet and crawled on her knees up into the middle of the mattress. The central air conditioning made sleeping under a sheet quite comfortable, but Jesse couldn't bring herself to lie down or turn out the lights. Finally, she allowed herself the luxury of just leaning against the nest of pillows at her back. She was so tired. She'd only close her eyes for a moment. She wouldn't turn out the light, not just yet...not until she accustomed herself to her old room again...and the shadows...and the night sounds in the country. She fell asleep within minutes, curled into a tight little ball. And, in spite of all her determination, she began to dream.

It was always the same—the instant knowledge that she wasn't alone, the awful smell of an unwashed body, the odor of alcohol, the rough ugly words...and the knife. Jesse moaned softly, tossing about as she lay uncovered in the middle of the bed, kicking weakly in her sleep. The moans became a plea for mercy, the plea became a cry, the cry a scream.

King was on his feet and inside her room before he fully realized he'd gotten out of bed. But he knew what was wrong with Jesse the instant her terrorized screams had pierced his sleep.

Hesitating no longer than the time it took him to reach her bed, he scooped Jesse up into his arms with a single motion and spoke her name aloud in a calm, soothing tone of voice. She was awake almost instantly. It took another moment before the tears came, but when they did, they were cleansing; washing away the nightmare King had put to an abrupt end.

"Is she all right?" Maggie asked, trying to mask the panic she'd felt as she heard Jesse's pitiful cry. She'd reached the room only seconds behind King and had seen the natural way he'd handled the tense situation.

Instinctively, he'd done the right thing. She took in the sight of the scantily clad girl, the big, half-dressed man holding her tightly, and squashed the thought that crept into her heart.

"She will be now," King said, lowering Jesse to the floor, refusing to relinquish his hold on her. "We've been through this before, haven't we, Jess?"

Tilting her chin back with the tip of his finger, he wiped away the last of her tears and sighed. "It's okay, Maggie. Go back to bed. I'll stay with her for a while. I should have anyway. She hasn't been alone since the attack and this was just to be expected."

"I'm sorry," Jesse whispered, as she leaned weakly against King's strength. She felt his heartbeat against the back of her head, and knew by the race of the rhythm that she'd frightened him as much as she'd frightened herself. "I seem to be saying that a lot lately, Maggie. You didn't know what you were letting yourself in for when you wanted me here, did you?"

The quiver in Jesse's voice and the vulnerability in her brimming eyes was enough for Maggie. Whatever it took to make her girl whole again was going to have to be all right.

"Don't be silly," she answered. "You're not a bother. You're family. Now, King, you go on and do whatever you've been doing to help our girl get through this."

She wiped at her eyes and pulled nervously at her long, gray braid, then bustled out of Jesse's bedroom, talking to herself as she disappeared down the hall.

"Whatever it takes…that's what we're going to do. Whatever it takes."

King took in her tear-strained face, the rumpled T-shirt, the bare legs beneath, and knew he was asking for trouble. But for Jesse's sake, he didn't have a choice.

"Come here to me," King beckoned in a husky voice, and took her with him across the hall. Turning back the covers on his king-sized bed, he pointed to the unused side and gruffly announced, "I'm not sleeping in your room. That bed's too damn short." He softened his words by the gentleness of his touch as he crawled between the sheets and pulled Jesse down beside him. "Now go to sleep, Jesse," he whispered, and gathered her stiff little body against him.

He felt a slight hesitance from her before fear overrode propriety. She backed into the curve of his body, relaxing with a shaky sigh as she felt the cool firmness of his long, muscular arms pull her against him.

"Thank you, King," she whispered, and drifted off to sleep.

Don't thank me yet, he thought with a silent groan, as the soft curves of her hips settled against his lower stomach. *I've got to get through this night a sane man.*

Turner's old rooster crowed twice before Jesse forced herself to open her eyes. It had been so long since she'd been awakened by anything other than alarm clocks that it took her a moment to re-orient herself. Last night came crashing rudely back. All the fear and terror of the night had ended simultaneously with being wrapped securely in King's tender grasp. She allowed herself the luxury of watching the first early rays of the sun catch in the gold-tipped hair on King's arms and reveled in the quiet strength emanating from him, even as he slept.

The weight of his arm across the flat of her stomach was only a little heavy and Jesse knew she would have gladly welcomed all of him in a way King would never imagine. She turned her head slightly and tried not to let the catch in her breath alert him as she watched him sleep. He was so beautiful. She smiled to herself. Men weren't supposed to be beautiful, but...tell that to her heart. She couldn't quit watching his mouth as he slept peacefully, unaware of her. It was slightly parted, and the thought of tasting the firm, full-cut lips was intoxicating. Her gaze wandered upwards toward the thick, dark lashes that lay fanned over his upper cheekbones and knew that they covered dark eyes that rarely missed anything. Hair lay in mussed abandon on his wide, sun-tanned forehead. She resisted the urge to gently comb it away from his face. Instead, she allowed herself to see King as few saw him; quiet and vulnerable.

But this was getting her nowhere and making her more than a bit miserable. Jesse sighed softly and stretched, trying to get enough incentive to move. Yet she didn't want to move, ever. This was exactly where she'd yearned to be for as long as she cared to remember. The only thing wrong with the picture was that she was here for all the wrong reasons. King was doing this out of love all right, just not the kind of love Jesse wanted from him.

She felt the strong, solid length of him, and his even, steady breathing. Carefully, so as not to alert him, she began to scoot from under his grasp. Even asleep, King sensed her movement and pulled her back against him. Jesse felt his hand splay over her stomach, then slide upward until he seemed to find a more comfortable spot. She held her breath as his hand wandered, then let her breath out slowly as his hand come to rest just under the soft, generous curves of her breasts. His sigh of satisfaction made quick tears come and go in Jesse's eyes and she blinked furiously, anxious that he not awaken to see her in this state.

She'd successfully hidden her true feelings for King for years, never allowing herself to dream that something such as this would ever come to pass. But now to be thrust in such close quarters for the wrong reasons was the epitome of irony.

Jesse closed her eyes, let imagination turn her in his arms, taste the sun-browned flavor of his muscular chest and work her way upwards with tiny kisses and nips until she reached the chiseled perfection of his mouth and welcomed King and the day together. The thought was intoxicating. She knew she had to move before the thought became deed.

Carefully, she lifted away the lightweight sheet covering them and slid her fingers gently over King's hand, reluctantly removing herself from his grasp. Allowing herself just one small luxury, she very gently brushed her lips across the hand that had held her safely through the night. Then she quietly scooted to the side of the huge bed and slipped from King's room without looking back.

He'd been awake since the moment her fingers touched his hand. He'd started to speak, and then something made him remain silent. An instinct...or curiosity...he didn't know which. But he hadn't moved. Nothing could have prepared him for the jolt that shot through him as Jesse's lips brushed across his fingers. Reflex made him clutch a handful of the bedsheet. He gritted his teeth to keep from calling her name—calling her back to his bed as she walked out the door.

"What in hell is happening to me?" King muttered aloud as he watched his body betray him.

Rolling over with a painful groan, he pressed his aching body into the unyielding mattress and knew it wasn't what he wanted under him. He also knew nothing was going to make the ache go away. He suspected it was only going to get worse.

Unwilling to face, or even investigate, his new feelings for Jesse, he chose his usual way of dealing with an out-of-control situation. He was going to ignore it. He crawled out of bed and headed for the shower.

"Just coffee," King growled in his husky rasp. "Not hungry."

Maggie's eyebrows shot skyward as she heard King speaking what she called "McCandless shorthand." It was a strange family trait that surfaced in times of stress or anger. Andrew...King...even Duncan had all exhibited varying degrees of the family trait. Maggie suspected all was not well in King's world. She also suspected Jesse had something to do with his cranky behavior.

"Good morning to you, too," Maggie said wryly. "Did someone get up on the wrong side of the bed?"

"Been a lot better off if I'd never gotten in the damn thing," King muttered into his coffee cup. Then he quickly swallowed a curse with the fiery gulp of steamy brew.

"It's hot," Maggie warned too late, and turned away so King would not see her smile.

"I'll be out most of the day," King said, and added as he started out the door, "Keep an eye on Jesse. I think she'll be fine...but..." he cautioned, remembering her flashback episode at the hospital. "If you need me, just find Turner. He'll know where I am."

"You'll miss Duncan," Maggie reminded him. "He said he'd be over today."

"Hell!" King muttered, and then mentally rearranged his earlier plans. He had every intention of being present when his uncle arrived. Something was going on between him and Jesse and he wanted to see for himself.

"I'll be in at noon," he said, leaning over to kiss Maggie's cheek, "in a better mood."

"Humpf," she replied, and watched him walk toward the horse barns, his long legs quickly covering the distance. Then he disappeared into the dark, cool depths of the airy building.

Chapter 5

Jesse mentioned virtually nothing of the preceding night's events, nor did she mention anything of the aftermath. She had been hiding her feelings for King for so long that it was second nature to be noncommittal.

She and Maggie worked side by side as they went about the daily chore of putting the huge, rambling ranch house to rights. They chattered idly, visiting about nothing in particular, yet it was obvious that the daily routine was becoming almost more than Maggie could handle alone. Jesse was certain King didn't realize the increasing difficulties Maggie faced daily. Each passing year added problems, none of which she could control. There were aching joints, a slower stride, and small moments of weariness that she could not hide, even from herself.

Jesse knew that she probably wouldn't have noticed the differences in Maggie if she hadn't been gone for such a long time. Coming back home now was like seeing everything and everyone for the first time.

"I might have known," Maggie said with a sigh, as she looked out the living room window she had just dusted. "Here comes Duncan just in time for lunch. I'll set another place."

Jesse looked about wildly, uncertain whether to follow Maggie to the kitchen and prolong the moment when she'd have to face Duncan, or stay and get it over with. She opted for the latter.

There was no time to change into something less revealing than the blue, terrycloth shorts and shirt she was wearing. It had been too hot to wear much else after the struggle she'd had with Maggie's vacuum cleaner. Jesse had insisted she was perfectly capable of using it. But the constant pull and push of the handle and the weight of the machine itself had almost been too much for her still tender hands.

Oh, well, she sighed, *I could be wearing a nun's habit and Duncan would still undress me with a single look. And I don't remember where I left my shoes.*

So, Jesse waited, defenseless to postpone the inevitable confrontation. She gritted her teeth as she heard him bounding up the front steps of the verandah, whistling some unrecognizable tune a bit off-key.

"Something smells wonderful," he shouted as he entered the house, paused in front of the mirror on the hall tree and smoothed his hand over his perfectly groomed hair.

"Duncan," Jesse said, as she came into the hallway holding out her hand in greeting. "It's been a while, hasn't it?"

The forced gaiety and exuberance fell from his demeanor like a deflated balloon. He'd known Jesse was here. He just hadn't expected her to initiate the meeting. He couldn't put into words what he was feeling. But it was something between anger and shame.

He kept remembering the last time he'd seen her. And after what had happened recently, he wasn't certain how to behave. Her outstretched hand couldn't be ignored. He slipped back into his bravado and sandwiched her offering of greeting between his hands in a none too gentle grasp. Instantly he remembered her injuries, but not soon enough to prevent her gasp of pain.

"Jesse, dear," he mumbled. "I'm so sorry. I didn't think. Here, let me look."

"No," Jesse argued. "It's all right," and tried to pull her hand away.

She struggled unsuccessfully as Duncan grasped one hand and then the other and turned them palm sides up. He couldn't hide the shudder that ran through his big frame as he gazed fully at the healing evidence of her ordeal.

"Your hands!" he whispered, and pulled them upwards to his lips. "Dear God! Your hands," he muttered again. "Said you weren't hurt. Lied..." he said brokenly, "lied."

"Duncan! Please!" Jesse struggled, and finally succeeded in pulling her hands away from his mouth. He was acting strangely. And his words made no sense.

"Lunch is about ready," she announced, and tried not to run toward Maggie and the kitchen area where she heard her working out obvious aggression on the pots and pans. "And," she added, unnecessarily, "King will be here soon."

It seemed that speaking his name would give her some measure of insurance against Duncan saying something that she didn't want to deal with, especially now.

Duncan was in shock. His feet were moving. He must be saying all the right things. But he couldn't for the life of him remember what he'd said. Seeing Jesse had brought back all too vividly the last time they'd been together. It was not a memory he liked to recall.

Jesse was experiencing a similar jolt of memory and wished, all too fervently, that this day would soon be over.

"So, Jesse's moving to St. Louis?" Duncan asked, barely controlling his glee at the news. Maybe, if he got her away from this damn ranch and his perfect nephew, he'd have a chance with her.

Duncan had seen, all too clearly, the way Jesse looked at King. He'd also been aware, long before the others at the ranch, that Jesse LeBeau was a very beautiful, desirable woman. And, since turning twenty-one, she was also a very well-to-do woman. All of the above were attributes Duncan McCandless felt absolutely necessary in a wife. He scoffed at working a nine-to-five job. He shouldn't have to. After all, he *was* a McCandless.

His periodic appearances at the oil company that Jesse's father, Michael, and his brother, Andrew, had founded, were none too well received. He was tolerated solely because he was a McCandless. He'd inherited a goodly portion of the company stock at Andrew's death. But the dividends were not enough to keep Duncan in the manner to which he'd accustomed himself. He was growing weary of trying to devise ways in which to make a quick buck. As far as he was concerned, Jesse was the answer to his prayers. All he had to do was court her and marry the rest of the money he felt was, by all rights, his anyway. Duncan also planned to capitalize on the likeness that existed between him and his nephew. After all, if she liked one man's looks, another so much alike should suffice. And King had his head in the clouds as far as Jesse LeBeau was concerned. His mind was on everything but romance. Duncan considered Jesse an easy mark.

Unfortunately for Duncan, Jesse saw way beyond the surface of both McCandless men. He would have never wasted his time and money had he known how repulsed Jesse actually was by all his posturing.

She'd only been in St. Louis a month when Duncan made his first move. His plans had been carefully orchestrated and the "chance" meeting between him and Jesse was a success.

Leaving the Double M had been difficult for Jesse. Then, when King had not called or written other than to satisfy himself that she'd arrived and settled in safely, she'd been devastated. She didn't realize King was simply giving her the space he thought she desired. Her decision to leave had been a shock. King and Maggie had finally come to the conclusion that she just wanted to be on her own for a while, and had made every effort not to intrude. Their lack of communication fell right in with Duncan's plans. His casual offer of dinner in had been eagerly accepted. It began his forays into the life of Jesse LeBeau.

The "chance" meeting escalated into a weekly visit that he purposely let seem entirely her decision. Jesse was lonely, and for a short while, was swayed by Duncan's charm and likeness to the man she loved.

But the weeks grew into months and King did not come. Jesse grew tired of pretending to herself that anything was going to change. All the while, Duncan maintained a manner with Jesse that could only be called gentlemanly. He was certain that it would only be a matter of months before she'd capitulate and all his plans would come to fruition.

But instead of falling in with Duncan's ideas, Jesse began to withdraw more and more. Finally even Duncan sensed his looming failure. That was when he made his mistake. Although she never returned the casual hug and kiss he gave her at the end of each visit, she didn't refuse them either. Duncan saw only dollar signs, not the signs of annoyance that Jesse struggled to disguise.

But Duncan's pressing financial problems and Jesse's obvious withdrawal escalated his carefully laid scheme. He'd refused her attempt to cancel their dinner engagement at one of St. Louis's finest restaurants after severe weather warnings. Instead, they'd arrived at the proposed time while the pouring rain slowly turned into icy pellets. Duncan had studiously ignored Jesse's worried glances outside the restaurant window until even he began to see the stupidity of staying longer. However, he had taken the bad turn in the weather as an opportunity he wasn't going to pass up.

"If you don't care for dessert, Jesse, dear," he said, slipping his hands over hers as she placed her napkin at the side of her plate, "I believe I'd better get you home. It seems the roads *are* getting worse, and I don't want to take any chances with your safety."

He leaned over in the circular booth they were sharing and slipped his hand under the collar of her sweater as he spoke, refusing to acknowledge the flash of distaste that clouded her eyes.

Jesse had been trying for several weeks to find a way to lessen the attention Duncan kept showing her. But she was at a loss. At first he'd been a welcome visitor—someone from home. Yet he always made Jesse slightly uncomfortable by the way he looked at her, and the practiced casualness of his touch. She'd tried to get out of this dinner all day. The weather was uncertain and she needed to average the grades of her students and have them ready to post on report cards when Christmas break was over. It *had* been a long, lonely holiday. Finally she'd weakened at Duncan's persistence.

"Yes," she eagerly agreed, as he suggested they leave. "I'm finished. And the roads look worse."

She was anxious to get home and away from Duncan. For some reason, she sensed something different about him. His behavior was making her uneasy. There was an almost desperate quality that she didn't like. She didn't like it at all.

The drive home took forever. The roads had worsened. They made it home safely due only to the fact that nearly everyone else had the good sense to stay indoors and off the roads.

Duncan saw Jesse to her door, bestowed his usual farewell, and quite off-handedly remarked he'd probably break his neck before he got back to his hotel.

Jesse felt a twinge of guilt, but remained stubbornly silent as she watched him get in his car and begin the hazardous job of backing down the slope of her icy driveway. Suddenly, before her eyes, Duncan's car spun in a complete circle and came to rest on the neighbor's yard. She opened the front door and stepped out, calling anxiously as she saw Duncan groggily shake his head.

"Duncan," she called, "are you hurt?"

He looked up at the sound of her voice, opened the door and stepped out with a huge smile on his face. He shrugged his shoulders as if to indicate his innocence in the whole proceedings and started walking carefully back toward Jesse's house.

"No, I'm not hurt," Duncan answered. "But it looks like you're stuck with me until morning. Hope you don't mind. I'll just stretch out on your sofa. You'll never know I'm here."

There was absolutely nothing Jesse could say to deny him entrance. She also didn't know that one of the few things Duncan could do well was handle a car. He'd been "shooting doughnuts" on the ice since he was a kid.

The next two hours went smoother than Jesse could have hoped. He was considerate and unobtrusive as she finished averaging and posting the student grades in her book. She heard Duncan moving quietly about in the kitchen, but the only obtrusion he made was to bring a pot of her favorite apple-scented tea and set it and a cup and saucer within reach. She looked up to thank him, but he was already gone.

Maybe I'm making more of this than I should, Jesse thought. *He's actually being true to his word.*

Finally her work was finished. Jesse slammed the pages of her grade book shut with a satisfied plop. She pushed her chair back and stretched her legs out before her, stood and wearily tilted her head from side to side, trying to work the kinks out of her neck and tired shoulder muscles.

"Need a back rub?" Duncan asked softly.

His voice startled her. She turned to see him watching her from the doorway of the den. Jesse shuddered.

She hadn't been aware of his presence and it made her uneasy.

"No, no. It's fine. A good night's sleep will take care of it," Jesse answered anxiously, hoping he would move away from the doorway so she could escape to relative safety in her bedroom. But Duncan was too big and compelling, and kept looking at her in a very unsettling way.

"Well," she said brightly, "if there's anything you need during the night, Duncan, please feel free to help yourself. Food, extra blankets, anything..."

"There is something I need Jesse, dear." He began walking slowly toward her. "No. Something I want."

Jesse's heart stopped and then raced. All speech left her as she began backing away from Duncan. But there was nowhere to go.

"Don't be afraid, my dear," he crooned. He slipped his hands on either side of her neck and cupped her face, tilting it toward his dark, fathomless gaze. "You know how I feel about you. You must! Please, let me show you how precious you are to me. Let me stay with you tonight. Let me take care of you, always."

"No...no," Jesse whispered, feeling revulsion at his touch. She struggled uselessly within his grip, and fought down the rising black tide of fear that threatened to overwhelm her. This couldn't be happening! She had to be dreaming, because this *was* a nightmare.

"You've misunderstood, Duncan. I don't think of you that way. You're Andrew's brother—King's uncle. I've always thought of you as family. Please!" And the last came out with a sob as she struggled wildly to get away from his lips on her neck...on her face...on her mouth. "Don't touch me!" she screamed, and pushed with both hands, pressing and hitting against his chest with all the strength she could muster. It wasn't much, but her struggles broke his grip and Jesse fell back with a choked cry.

She wrapped her arms around herself, trying to keep the nausea that was boiling in her stomach at bay. She no longer hid the repulsion she felt in his presence.

Duncan's eyes narrowed, and an ugly smile came and went on his handsome face.

"What's the matter, princess?" he sneered. "Aren't I good enough for you? Or am I not what you wanted after all? Let me guess...the princess wants the King, not the jester. Am I right?"

Jesse gasped, suddenly aware of how defenseless and alone she was...and just how angry Duncan was.

"Get out!" she ordered, drawing strength from deep within. She pointed her finger in his face and began advancing toward him. She wouldn't be afraid...not in her own home. "Go home, Duncan."

Unconsciously Duncan backed away, surprised by her vehemence, but the ugly smile and threat in his demeanor remained. He wasn't prepared to give up on this woman and her money this easily. He was too desperate.

"You forgot about the weather," he reminded her with a gleam in his eyes. "I can't leave yet. It's too dangerous."

"No, Duncan," Jesse said ominously. "Not as dangerous as it will be if you stay here. Get out! Get out now…or I'll tell King."

She couldn't have made more of an impact if she'd slapped him. His easy way of life depended on staying within his nephew's graces.

"Damn you," he whispered, as he grabbed his coat and gloves from the table in her living room. "One day you'll be sorry, princess. One day you'll be very sorry!"

Jesse held her breath as he slammed the door suddenly behind him. She quickly locked the door and then sank limply onto the living room sofa. Her eyelids teared and she blinked furiously. Duncan was gone. She had nothing to cry about. Then she lowered her head to her knees and cried herself to sleep.

"Lunch is ready," Maggie announced to Jesse, as she practically ran into the kitchen. She raised her eyebrows, but judiciously said nothing, as Duncan entered right behind Jesse with an odd expression on his face. Maggie knew there was old trouble between them but kept her thoughts to herself.

"I'll go get King," Jesse offered breathlessly, and gave neither Maggie nor Duncan a chance to object. She exited the kitchen on the run.

"You better put on some shoes," Maggie called, but it was too late. Jesse was gone. "Here," she said, as she placed a stack of plates in Duncan's hands. "You can set the table." She ignored his look of outrage and surprise and turned back to her pots and pans. It wouldn't hurt him to earn his meal for a change.

The hot, loose dust in the driveway made tiny poofs between Jesse's bare toes as she hurried toward the horse barns. The thick, sweet scent of honeysuckle along the backyard fence wafted through the air, and Jesse inhaled deeply, satisfied, in spite of the heat, to be away from the cloying atmosphere inside the ranch house. A daring little sweet bee lit on the back curve of Jesse's thigh and then quickly lifted off just before her hand reached him.

Jesse squinted her eyes against the glare of the noon-day sun and stopped for a moment in the shade of one of the red oaks lining the long driveway of the Double M. She held her breath and listened, then turned with a smile toward the gleaming white stalls where King's brood mares were kept. She could hear him, even from here, issuing a short, decisive order to one of the hands. A horse's neigh pierced the air in objection as men's voices continued to call back and forth to one another. Jesse rounded the corner and slipped silently into the welcome depths of the cool, airy barns that opened at both ends to capture the maximum flow of air.

A shiny, red king cab pickup truck pulling a matching air-conditioned horse trailer was backed into the barn area. It was obvious that King had just sold some of his stock.

She watched as a young filly and two colts, part of his herd of two-year olds, were carefully loaded into the comfortable depths of the long trailer. She couldn't hide her admiration at the way they responded to King's handling. The beauty and clean lines of their distinctive build, their long, delicate legs, the magnificent width of their chests and long, flowing manes and tails belied the spirit and endurance for which the true Arabians were bred. She knew King suffered mixed feelings each time he had to part with his stock. Although that was why he raised him, selling them was always a difficult hurdle to pass.

King carefully led the last of the young horses into the trailer and then stepped back, allowing the men to remove the loading ramp and fasten the end gate of the trailer securely. It was only after he watched to assure himself that the truck and trailer had successfully cleared the barn opening that he spied Jesse standing in the shadows. He began walking toward her.

Jesse saw him wave and smile, then saw a frown appear on his face and knew why before he got within shouting distance.

"Lunch is ready," she said, hoping she could sidetrack his train of thought. It didn't work.

"Where the hell are your shoes?" he growled, and glared fiercely at the wide, blue eyes staring back at him with feigned innocence.

This was an old battle they'd fought for years. Jesse knew it was only for her own safety that he continually cautioned her, but she loved the feel of going barefoot. And at the age of twenty-five, she was unlikely to change.

"Come on," Jesse chided, ignoring his bluffed anger. She hurried toward the ranch house, assuming he would follow. "Maggie's waiting."

King narrowed his eyes and tried to ignore the gentle movement of her breasts under the skimpy little blue top she was wearing, but didn't succeed. Then he realized she had nothing on under it. That made things even worse. The sexy sway of her hips in the matching shorts did nothing to help the increasing pressure behind the zipper of his Levi's, and he cursed roundly under his breath as he hurried to catch up. Maybe if he walked beside her and not behind it would turn his mind to a safer channel.

"You didn't answer me, Jesse," he said, as his husky voice broke the silence between them. "You know not to come barefoot around the barns." Then his voice grew gentle, and he slid his hand along her arm, tightening on her wrist as he pulled her to a stop and made her face him. Her quiet statement blew everything else from his mind.

"Duncan is here," she said.

King felt her pulse jump beneath his fingers, and he sighed in frustration. He'd wanted to be present at the first meeting between them. He didn't know exactly why, but he suspected there was an old, unsettled problem he should know about. Yet he was uncertain about how to get the information from Jesse. She could be so damn hardheaded.

"And," she continued, gently pulling her wrist from his grasp, "I'll try to be more careful. I promise."

King didn't know whether she meant she'd be more

careful about where she went barefoot, or more careful around Duncan. But it was too late to ask as Maggie's impatient voice hurried them both inside.

King quickly washed and changed into a fresh shirt, brushed most of the dust and grass from his pant legs, and hurried to the table. He'd kept them waiting too long. It didn't pay to pull this stunt with Maggie many times. She'd fed leftovers to the barn cats more than once rather than put up with tardiness at the table. He'd eaten dozens of baloney sandwiches because of it.

The food was good, the cool comfort of the house a welcome relief, and the conversation was casual and very ordinary. Yet King had never sat through a more uncomfortable meal in his life. Maggie talked on and on about the weatherman's repeated daily warnings of fire danger due to the extreme drought. Duncan alternated between charming Maggie and looking at Jesse with an expression King felt almost obliged to punch off his face. He reluctantly decided that would not be wise, and sat silently, fuming over a situation he didn't understand.

Jesse blithely refused to look at either Duncan or King. Instead, she talked too much about absolutely nothing. King didn't know whether to shout or leave in disgust. The decision was shelved as the shrill peal of the telephone startled the quartet around the table.

"I'll get it," Jesse offered, anxious to get away from the antagonistic atmosphere hanging over the table. She scooted her chair back so quickly, King didn't even have time to blink as she grabbed the wall phone by the kitchen cabinets.

King watched the expression on her face change to one of disbelief and then terror. He debated with himself for about half a second until he saw her chin quiver. That was all it took. He rose from his chair with a violent move and grabbed the phone from her hand.

"Who the hell is this?" he asked. But the voice that answered him was not what he'd expected.

He sighed as he pulled Jesse gently into his arms, and absently rubbed his thumb against a tiny mole behind her ear. The ill-concealed elation of Captain Shockey's voice and the message he had for them were what they'd all been waiting for, yet at the same time, fearing would come.

"Do you have him in custody?" King asked, and then turned and frowned at Duncan as he abruptly stood upright, knocking his chair over backward with a loud bang. He turned away too soon and missed the look of pure panic that accompanied his uncle's odd behavior.

"Okay," King said, after listening to Captain Shockey's request. "I want to propose an alternate solution to this new turn of events. Since all you have at this time are pictures, couldn't you send copies to the Tulsa police department so Jesse can view them there? I don't think she's up to a trip back to St. Louis just yet."

King felt the breath leave Jesse's body as she stood

stiffly beneath his hands, waiting anxiously for an answer to King's request.

"Great!" King said. "That's even better. And Shockey," he said after a pause, "thanks."

He hung up the phone and turned to face his waiting audience.

"The St. Louis police, acting on a tip from a store clerk, think there's a good possibility that their suspect was caught on videotape as he entered and exited their store. They are sending a copy of the tape here for Jesse to see. You don't have to go back to St. Louis sweetheart. You don't even have to go to Tulsa." He felt her relaxing against him. "It's going to be okay."

"Well, that's wonderful news, isn't it, Maggie." Duncan said loudly, and reached down to set his chair upright. "I've got to be running along now. Thanks for the meal. And, Jesse…it was good to see you again. Take care." He disappeared.

"Well," Maggie muttered. "Easy come, easy go." Then she turned and pointed at Jesse's drawn countenance. "And you, my dear, are due a rest. I don't want any argument. King…" she pointed again, including him in her orders. "See that she minds for a change."

Jesse stifled a sob, threw her arms around Maggie's neck, and kissed the mass of tiny wrinkles on her cheek.

"I love you," Jesse whispered in her ear. "And I almost always mind you." Then, ignoring Maggie's snort, she let King lead her from the kitchen.

"Are you all right?" he asked softly, as he watched

carefully for any signs of undue stress. He didn't want another flashback episode.

"Yes," she answered. "Thanks for helping me. I don't know what made me freeze up. Hearing Captain Shockey's voice made everything come crashing back. For a few hours today, I almost let myself believe that everything was more or less back to normal. The phone call was just a bitter reminder of how I'd been fooling myself."

King struggled with the urge to kiss every tiny frown that lined her forehead and made the usual tilt of her mouth droop with despair. The more he was around her, the more he had to struggle to keep his hands off. He didn't know what was happening to him, but he knew whatever he was feeling for Jesse had nothing to do with pity.

"Would you mind running me a bath, King? I'm too sticky and dusty to sleep on anything but the back porch unless I clean up."

King made himself ignore the touch of her hand on his arm and refused to meet her eyes. He shoved his hands deep in the front pockets of his Levi's and muttered, more harshly than he meant to, "Just use my shower. I've got to get back to the stables. There's another buyer due soon and I don't want to be late."

He backed out of her doorway and had to force himself not to run away from the stunned look on her face. He knew he'd sounded harsh and impatient, but showing his true feelings at a time like this didn't seem prudent. *Hell!* he thought as he walked aimlessly toward the barns. *I don't even know what my true feelings are.*

Jesse felt quick tears fill her eyes at the harshness of his voice and his hasty exit. She'd known this "coming home" thing wouldn't work from the beginning. Unfortunately, for her own safety, she had no choice. No one saw her leaden steps, or the droop of her shoulders, as she pushed the door to his room open and quietly closed it behind her.

It was late afternoon when King looked up from the rail he'd been nailing firmly back on the corral fence by the barn. He saw a cloud of dust coming closer and closer down the long driveway and frowned. He pulled an already damp handkerchief from his hip pocket and halted the salty beads of moisture on his forehead just before they slipped into his eyes. Then his heart quickened, and his feet began to move toward the ranch house before his brain told him why they should. It was the familiar shape of the white, four-door sedan and the long antenna whip on the back of the vehicle identifying it as a police car that made the hair on the back of his neck stand on end. He realized it would be another sleepless night.

"Hell of a deal," the sheriff said, as he solemnly greeted King. He'd known the McCandless family for years, and held them in high regard. He had a daughter near Jesse LeBeau's age, and knew how he would feel in similar circumstances. He hadn't known of the attack on Jesse until he'd received the phone call and instructions from St. Louis. Later the same day, the special express package he now carried firmly in his grasp had arrived, and he knew what he had to do.

"How's she doing, King?" he asked.

"It's been rough on her, Sheriff. But she's a survivor. She had to be or she wouldn't be here today. I just hope to hell this is the man. I want the bastard behind bars."

The sheriff nodded in understanding and followed King into the house.

"Have a seat," King indicated with a sweep of his hand, as he ushered the sheriff into the den where a television and VCR rested on the shelf of the entertainment center. "Maggie will bring you something cool to drink. I've got to go find Jesse."

A quick word to Maggie produced the answer to Jesse's whereabouts, and he went toward the bedroom wing while Maggie fixed the promised refreshments.

King knocked softly on Jesse's door. Nothing and no one seemed to be stirring. He knocked again a bit sharper. After receiving no response again, he pushed the door open, expecting to see Jesse sound asleep on her bed.

The room was dark, the shades pulled against the glare of the hot July sun, and he blinked a moment, giving his eyes time to adjust to the change of light. When he was finally able to see, he frowned. The room was empty. King wiped a weary hand across his face and decided to freshen up before he went looking elsewhere. He didn't have far to go.

Jesse was curled up in the middle of his bed. Even

in the deepest of sleeps, she hugged his pillow against her chest and face as King had held her against him the night before. The loose cotton shift she was wearing was twisted and bunched high above her knees and gave King much too much leg to try and ignore.

"God give me strength," he muttered softly, and walked over to the side of his bed. He felt his breath catch in his throat and had to swallow twice before he could say her name. Finally it came out in a husky growl.

"Jesse, you better wake up, girl, or you'll never sleep tonight."

His teasing voice penetrated her dreamless slumber, and she smiled into her pillow before rolling over on her back, stretching lazily against the teak-colored comforter on his bed.

"Hi," she said slowly, and a soft, gentle smile creased her lips as she stretched her hands above her head, pulling her shift a tiny bit higher.

King didn't even know he'd moved. But he suddenly found himself on his hands and knees, straddling her bare legs as he braced his hands on the mattress on either side of her shoulders.

"You lost?" he whispered, and gently pushed a dark, wavy lock of hair from her eyes.

Jesse forgot to breathe. Her eyes widened and she knew her heartbeat could probably be heard in Tulsa. *Please don't let this be a dream,* she thought, and refused to move a muscle for fear the dream would vanish.

"No, I'm not lost," she finally answered, and looked long and hard, trying to read the expression in King's eyes. "I'm never lost when I'm with you."

Her words hit him in the stomach with fist force. "Oh, honey," he whispered, and leaned forward, gently tasting the sleep-softened expression on her mouth.

The touch was fleeting. The taste just a hint of what lay beneath him if he only dared take it. He raised up, leaning back until he was sitting on the back of his bootheels and felt as if he were being sucked up into the vortex of a storm. He doubled his hands into fists and pressed them fiercely into his knees to keep from touching her again. If he moved, he was afraid the next time he wouldn't stop with a taste of Jesse LeBeau.

Jesse closed her eyes as she saw him coming closer and was finally convinced she wasn't dreaming as King's lips met hers. It may as well have been a branding iron. The sensation was no less a mark of possession in her heart. Every inch of her skin felt alive, every beat of her heart in tune with his own. Just as she started to lock her hands behind his head and pull him closer, he moved away. Jesse had to force herself not to cry aloud at the pain she experienced, or at the distance once again between them.

She watched in wide-eyed silence while he seemed to struggle with some overwhelming emotion, and wondered as she watched, why he had so suddenly stopped. Finally she could no longer wait, and gently ventured a touch on his leg and hand.

"King?" she began, but was never allowed to finish.

Jesse's voice startled King. It brought him back to reality with a painful jolt.

"Hellfire," he muttered. "I completely forgot why I was looking for you."

He rolled off the bed with one motion, and stood silently, holding out his hand for her to join him.

Jesse blinked in confusion, and then reached upward. King gently pulled her from his bed.

"What?" she asked, trying to make sense of the mixed signals she was receiving from King. Then she couldn't mask the shudder as he spoke.

"The sheriff is here with the tape, Jesse. He needs for you to take a look at the suspect. Come on, honey. They're waiting for us in the den."

"Just give me a minute," she mumbled, and started toward her room. "Oh," she added, trying to blink away the tears in her eyes. "You didn't have to break the news to me so gently, King." Jesse had deciphered his actions as nothing more than gentle consideration. "I'm not going to fall apart again. I promise."

King stood in stunned silence and let Jesse walk away. He felt unable to move or speak. He didn't know whether to be glad or sorry that she'd misinterpreted what had just happened on his bed. Finally, all he could do was curse himself roundly and hurry to the waiting group in the den.

Chapter 6

Night sounds kept teasing at Jesse's concentration as she fought the sheet twisted around her legs. She'd spent every moment since her head touched the pillow trying uselessly to block out the image of the man on the videotape. Her mental state upon entering the den had not been the best, thanks to what had—or had not—transpired between her and King. She watched the first few frames of the video without actually seeing anything.

Suddenly the man in question had turned and the camera caught him full face. Jesse gasped loudly and took a few steps backward in shocked recognition.

"It's him," she cried, and turned around wildly in the partially darkened room, half expecting him to materialize.

King had been carefully watching her face for signs of recognition. He knew the moment Jesse connected with the image before her. He saw her panic and caught her backward progress before hysteria had time to set in.

Jesse was frantic. Her frightened blue eyes brimmed with unshed tears as she grabbed King by the forearms, trying to shake him into believing her.

"King! It's him. I know it! That's the man who tried to kill me!"

"Are you certain, Jesse?" the sheriff asked. "You couldn't possibly be mistaken?"

"No!" she shouted, and shrugged out of King's protective grasp. "I saw that man as 'up close and personal' as I've ever seen anyone in my life." Then her voice lost it's sarcasm and the adrenaline in her system began to subside. "You don't quickly forget the man who tries to kill you, Sheriff. You've got to tell Captain Shockey. They've got to find him! Find him quick! Then I'll be safe. Then he won't hurt me…or anyone else again."

She sank limply onto the arm of an easy chair and buried her face in her hands. "Turn off the tape. I can't look anymore."

"I'll make the call from here," the sheriff said, gesturing toward the phone on King's desk.

In a matter of minutes, after passing on Jesse's confirmation to the St. Louis police department, the sheriff also discovered they already had a name and address for the man in the video. They had simply been waiting for Jesse's verification before getting a search and arrest warrant. The phone call was short, the news something of a relief. Finally a name and a face had been added to the case.

"Wiley Lynch," Jesse muttered. "A man named Wiley Lynch tried to kill me." She turned away from her stance by the window and asked poignantly of no one in particular, "Why?"

Maggie looked away, unable to find words to help Jesse.

King started toward her but was stopped by a look from Jesse as she quickly turned away, unwilling to see the pity on their faces. She stumbled from the den.

Jesse heard the sheriff leave and heard Maggie and King's hushed voices. She knew they were talking about her, and quietly slipped out the back door. She'd had enough turmoil for one day. She had let herself believe that King actually felt something for her. Then, after discovering he was only trying to break the news of the sheriff's arrival as gently as possible, her world had fallen the rest of the way in on top of her. The sight of the man who'd tried to kill her was the final touch to an otherwise horrendous day.

She sought solace in Turner's company and actually found herself enjoying the evening chores that she helped him finish. He didn't know what had just transpired, and treated her as if everything in her life was back to normal. It was just what she needed. King and Maggie hovered too much, although she knew it was done out of love. There was only so much sheltering possible. Part of this nightmare was for Jesse alone.

Getting through the awkward silences during dinner wore her out. Jesse quickly excused herself and left King and Maggie to themselves. She didn't want any help and she didn't want to talk to King. Finally she'd given up trying to outwait the sunrise and gone to bed. But sleep wouldn't come.

Jesse kicked the sheet from her legs in frustration and sat straight up in bed. She leaned over, turned on the table lamp, and ran her fingers roughly through her hair. She couldn't sleep and she wasn't seeking solace in King's arms, or in his bed, again. There was only so much she could endure, and the limit was imminent.

In a matter of seconds, she'd slipped out of her night shirt, into a pair of old gym shorts, and a tattered midriff-length T-shirt. She had to get some air. Maybe then her mind would slow down and let her get some rest. Jesse started toward the door and then stopped. She walked back to her closet and pulled out a pair of canvas deck shoes.

"Not at night, Jesse girl," she said to herself, unwilling to chance stepping on a scorpion or a snake, both common Oklahoma nightcrawlers.

She walked quickly and quietly through the house, sure of her direction and destination because of years and years of past residence, and because Maggie never re-arranged furniture.

The screen door squeaked just a bit as Jesse slipped outside the back door. She stood on the porch, inspecting the moonlit yard and shadows for things that didn't belong there. Satisfied that all was as it should be, she stepped off the porch and sighed in satisfaction as a faint, but steady breeze lifted the hair from her neck.

King awoke, sudden and swift, and lay silently for several seconds, trying to determine what, if anything, had called him from his tangled dreams. He listened, half expecting to hear sounds coming from Jesse's room. And then, when another faint but familiar sound filtered into his room, he hit the floor running, grabbing pants and boots in succession.

Jesse's room was empty. He pulled on his jeans and boots, stopping only long enough to stomp first one boot and then the other on sockless feet. He recognized the sound he'd heard. It was the squeaky hinge on the back door. Where in hell was she going?

Jesse had been so withdrawn since the sheriff's arrival it was beginning to worry him. He feared that the stress she kept suffering would cause another flash-back, or some other kind of set-back. He didn't know how to help her. She wouldn't talk and she wouldn't let him touch her.

But he feared it wasn't all due to the arrival of the tape. King also feared that his waking her and then actually crawling into bed with her had either frightened or repulsed her. He didn't know whether to say anything or just let it pass. If he made too much of the incident, it might embarrass Jesse further. The trouble was, King didn't quite know what to make of his actions either. He'd been more surprised than Jesse when he'd found himself on top of her. No wonder she wouldn't look him in the eye. He didn't know what she was thinking or feeling, but in some vague way he felt he'd let her down.

He hurried out the door and just caught a glimpse of her shirt before she disappeared around the curve in the driveway leading to the barns. He sighed with relief as he saw the direction she'd taken and knew where she was going. *Now,* he thought as he followed closely behind, *what in hell am I going to say to her when I get there?*

The barn was dark, light coming only from the doorways and the huge open window in the loft where hay was loaded and stored. The smells were comforting and familiar to Jesse. She leaned her head back against the wall and let old memories assail her. The faint but unmistakable scent of dry manure was nearly undetectable because of the fresher, aromatic bales of prairie hay, sacks of sweet feed for the horses, and the tang of well-oiled leather. Jesse knew exactly where she was, even with her eyes closed. She's spent the better portion of her life on the Double M with Andrew, then with King and the horses. A horse nickered softly, and Jesse smiled, knowing it probably sensed her presence. But it wasn't the stalls she was concerned with tonight. Tonight she wanted back a better, happier time in her life, and she knew where to find it. Up, above the earthen floor of the barn was a place—her place—and she needed desperately to find it—for the peace of mind it might still offer.

Jesse walked slowly but surely in the dim shadows towards the steps fastened firmly up the back wall of the barn leading to the loft. She knew that if there was a good breeze, it would come through that big opening above the ground floor where the bales of hay lay stacked like a grass castle. She grasped the steps firmly, wincing slightly as her hands closed over the rough wooden planks. Hand over hand she climbed, carefully placing her feet in firm positions as she advanced upward until her head poked through the opening in the loft floor. She paused, looked around in satisfaction, and pulled herself the rest of the way through the opening.

It was just as she remembered, a private world of hay, moonlight, and dreams that danced across the handhewn planks on the floor. Jesse took several tentative steps forward and then turned in delight in the center of a moonbeam as if it was a spotlight and she a soloist on a stage. She'd done it as a child and become lost in the fantasy, but tonight the fantasy wouldn't come. Jesse sighed and felt a deepening sadness as she watched the motes of dust she'd disturbed with her little dance settle back in place on the loft floor. Maybe it didn't work after you grew up. Maybe it didn't was because you had to believe in dreams. It hurt too much when dreams die, and today Jesse had felt the last of her dreams of a life with King helplessly disappear. The pain was more than she could bear. She sank limply to the floor.

"What am I going to do?" Jesse whispered aloud, and then let the pain engulf her.

King heard her moving around on the floor above and stepped aside just as a tiny shower of dust and bits of hay filtered down through the cracks of the floor. He knew what a special place the old hayloft had been to Jesse in the past, and suspected she had run to it now as a place of refuge. He debated about the wiseness of disturbing her and started to leave, allowing her the much needed time for solace. It was the muffled sobs spilling into the silence of the night that stopped his exit. He couldn't make himself leave her like this. Quietly he climbed up the steps and was standing in the shadows of the loft before Jesse knew he was present.

Sobs shook her fragile shoulders as she sat curled in upon herself. A cloud passed over the face of the moon, then cleared, bathing Jesse in a translucent glow so bright she seemed to be carved from marble. King watched, worried and confused. This sadness was not fear. It was despair.

A sudden thought struck him dumb and kept his feet stationary as he admitted to himself that he was the only other thing that could have possibly upset her today. At last, he knew he was going to have to face Jesse and make her talk to him as they should have talked long ago. He spoke her name.

The sound of his voice above and behind her made Jesse jump to her feet in shock.

"What are you doing here?" she asked angrily.

"Please, Jesse," he pleaded, and started toward her with outstretched hands. "Don't cry, honey. Talk to me. Whatever it is, you know I'll help. Is it something I've done? If it is, just tell me now! I can't stand to hear you cry."

"Stop right there!" she ordered, quickly wiping away tear tracks with the palms of her hands. "I don't want you here." Her voice shook. She could barely speak above a whisper as she continued. "You can't take away all my problems, King. You can't change what has happened to me, and you can't solve everything that goes wrong in my life. Besides," she accused, "where were you for the last three years? I took care of myself, by myself. Where were you King? Where were you?"

Her accusation hit him full force, and left him standing speechless and oddly ashamed. Then, he took a deep breath and threw the accusation back in her face.

"Where was I, Jesse? Right where you left me, girl. And you tell me this...and you tell me now," he said with a husky growl. "Why did you leave the Double M, Jesse Rose? Why did *you* leave me?"

His question staggered her, and she turned quickly away, unwilling for him to see her shock, afraid he would read the truth in her eyes. She stumbled toward the stacked bales of hay and started to climb... upward...anywhere...just as long as she didn't have to face King with answers she wasn't prepared to give.

"No, you don't, girl," he growled, grabbing both

her ankles before she could climb another bale. "Get down before you fall and hurt yourself."

Jesse stopped and turned slowly, knowing full well that King wouldn't loosen the firm grip he had on her legs. And so they stood, silently assessing each other's mood and determination.

"You're hurting my leg," Jesse finally said, and watched the pupils in his eyes darken and dilate with emotion. She knew he was angry at her. It wasn't often that he was met with the kind of resistance that Jesse kept throwing at him.

But it wasn't anger that Jesse saw in King's eyes. It was passion, the likes of which he'd never experienced. The feel of her skin beneath his hands was skyrocketing through his brain. He knew that her skin would be even softer in secret places.

He looked up at her tear-streaked face, and then down at his hands wrapped securely around her delicate ankles and shuddered, struggling with the urge to let both hands roam up the long, delicate curves of her calves, feel the little indentations he knew were behind her knees, and test the softness of the skin on her thighs. He couldn't get his mind off the thought of what lay above and beyond, and only steel-rimmed determination kept him from following his dreams. The sound of Jesse's voice drew him back, and he frowned at the disgruntled tone of her voice.

"Are you going to keep me here all night?" Jesse muttered, and struggled futilely with the iron grip he had on her legs.

I'd like to keep you here forever. King blinked, and wondered if he'd just said the thought aloud. He decided he had not, because Jesse seemed still to be waiting for an answer.

"Come here," he growled, and narrowed his eyes, daring her to move farther away. He slowly released his hold on her legs and held up his hands. She still had to descent from the stacked hay and King grasped her firmly under her arms and lifted her down.

Jesse leaned forward, knowing that he would catch her, and let him take the full brunt of her weight. She felt the sides of her breasts brush against his outstretched hands, watched his jaw clinch and the planes of his face harden as the muscles tightened beneath his skin. Jesse felt breath leave her body as he pulled her down against his bare chest. Every angle, every bulge, every heartbeat was magnified, as her body slid slowly down his entire length. His feet were planted firmly, using the strength of his heavily muscled legs to brace them both. Jesse slid right down to the space between.

She couldn't resist the urge to test the feel of the muscles encasing the heart she heard beating against her cheek, and let her hand lightly caress the breadth of his chest before she drew her hand away, letting her sense of smell and sight continue to touch King in a way she dared not.

She saw a line of moisture beginning to form in the cleft in the middle of his chest before it gained in strength and became droplets that would slide toward his flat muscled stomach, past the brass buttons on the waist of his Levi's and beyond to...

She shuddered, then inhaled, trying to regain her composure, and was inundated by the scents of soap, a woodsy, pine fresh scent from his shampoo, the ever-present smell of good leather, and the other, more un-definable scent of King, the man. She felt his heartbeat, the pulse racing beneath her fingertips, and knew he was feeling something, if only anger. She wanted to look at him...hoping...praying that she would see more in his eyes than she felt under his skin. But she resisted the urge and didn't move.

King forgot to breathe. When he did, it came out in a low groan as she slid slowly, slowly against every yearning, aching muscle in his body. When she put out her hand and touched the heartbeat beneath his chest, every muscle in his body tightened at once. He felt like a piece of coiled steel and knew it would take only the slightest touch from Jesse before he came unwound. She looked so soft and fragile, but King knew the strength and power in her. She would be a match for any man. He felt her hesitate and begin to pull away. The sensation was actually painful.

"No," he whispered before he thought, and slid his hands around her waist.

"What?" Jesse asked, her heart beginning to pound louder and louder in her ears. She knew if she said more it would be too much. Then he would know what she'd spent years trying to hide. She couldn't endure his rebuff. She wanted to love him—not this…and not in anger. "No what?" she insisted.

"Don't go." It came out somewhere between an order and a plea.

"Why?" she persisted, her heart racing with every breath she took, her body trembling beneath the possessive touch of his hands. "What *brotherly* advice could you possibly have for me at this time of night, King McCandless?"

Her voice taunted, the words teased, and King felt himself losing the fragile grip he had on reality as their sibling-like relationship was thrown back in his face.

"I'm not your damn brother," he growled, and pulled her up against the aching fullness of his body. "And, what I want to give you, Jesse, has nothing to do with advice."

"Dear God," Jesse whispered, and felt her legs beginning to give way at the picture his words drew in her mind.

Jesse knew the power between them was growing, and she knew that if she didn't stop this, he'd take her here and now, on the dusty floor of the loft, and never forgive her for letting it happen.

"King," she whispered, allowing his hands to venture farther and farther upward beneath the worn softness of her shirt, to the warmth and fullness of the soft, bare skin on her breasts.

"What?" he muttered, barely able to focus and answer her. The sensation of holding Jesse in such an intimate way was driving everything but need farther and farther away.

"I asked you first," she said, and felt his attention catch at the strangeness of her words.

"Asked me what?" he repeated, lost at the turn of conversation.

"Where were you the last three years of my life? Why didn't you come to St. Louis, King? Duncan came...why didn't you?"

Her voice broke, and the sadness of her words overwhelmed him. It was only after he found himself standing alone in the pale beam of moonlight by the window, watching from above as Jesse slowly made her way back to the ranch house alone, that her last words soaked into his consciousness. And when they did, it was too late. Too late to call her back. Too late to stop the jealousy and rage that sent him to his knees.

A light gray, nondescript sedan pulled into the narrow tree-lined driveway, and then stopped suddenly as a young boy darted across the driveway on a bicycle.

The man behind the wheel of the car and the boy on the bicycle looked at each other in stunned silence, each thanking their own luck for the near miss. Then the man rolled the car window down and frowned as a fly darted in through the opening.

"Damn!" he muttered, knowing he'd ride with that fly the rest of the day. "Hey, kid!" he called. "You better be more careful. You could get hurt pulling a stunt like that." He took the wide-brimmed Stetson off his head and wiped at the sweaty place along his forehead where it fit too snugly. He needed a haircut. Then his hat wouldn't fit so tight.

The boy watched wide-eyed, and then remembered where he'd been going in all his excitement.

"Thanks, mister," he yelled. "I'll be careful." He pointed up the driveway in an excited tone of voice. "You going up there with the other cops?" he asked, deciding that this man was a sheriff because of his cowboy hat.

"What cops?" the man asked suddenly, looking around with extreme interest.

"The ones up at the drunk's place. They been there since daylight. But Petey, who lives in the house by me, says no one was inside when the cops busted down the door. I'm going to see. I want to be a cop when I grow up." He puffed out his skinny little chest with importance.

"Say, kid," the cowboy called, but got nowhere since the boy began riding off on his bicycle, yelling over his shoulder as he pedaled away.

"I got to go. And I'm not supposed to talk to strangers."

Curses filled the car as the man slammed the hat back on his head and shut himself in with the fly. He backed carefully out of the drive and quickly drove away.

"At least he was gone," he muttered, and wondered what to do next. He knew he had to find Lynch before the police. Wiley Lynch would sell his mother for a drink. There was no way he'd keep his mouth shut about the LeBeau episode. He headed back to his motel to make some phone calls.

"This *was* the right place," one of the officers said to Captain Shockey. "We couldn't be more than six hours behind him." They were judging the time of Lynch's departure by the state of food scraps left on the kitchen table.

Shockey nodded his head, while his sharp little eyes scanned the place for something...anything...to confirm his growing suspicion that Lynch had not acted alone. He was a meticulous investigator, thorough in details that were not always popular with his staff, but invariably paid off in uncovering vital clues to his cases. Right now he had the men going through every piece of clothing, every piece of garbage inside and outside the house. Lynch had obviously not paid his city bills for several weeks and services, including garbage pickup, had been disconnected. There was quite an accumulation of the stuff, and it was hot as blazes in the house. It stunk to high heaven.

The search had been in progress for nearly an hour when one of the officers outside the back door shouted. There was something...a tone of voice Shockey recognized, and his adrenaline began to flow. He'd known this would pay off. Lynch was obviously not a smart criminal. He'd already made two serious mistakes. He was bound to make others. The second mistake he'd made was getting caught on videotape after passing a hot check. The first was ever breaking into Jesse LeBeau's house.

"Captain," the officer said, barely suppressing the excitement in his voice as he carefully opened an old, stained duffle bag and pulled a crumpled piece of paper from inside the torn lining. He held the paper with something that looked like long tweezers to keep from damaging the evidence, and carefully handed it to Shockey.

"Look at what I found inside this bag. I wouldn't have even seen it, but I thought the stains on the bag might possibly be blood stains. I checked closer, and this was caught in the lining."

"I knew it," Shockey muttered, as he turned the paper for a better look. The carefully clipped letters from newspaper print spelled certain guilt for Wiley Lynch. "I knew there was more to this than a random break-in! This is a ransom note! He was trying to kidnap her. If she hadn't resisted…if she hadn't fought…" Then his train of thought sharpened and he focused again. "Good work!" he said. "Get this to the lab immediately, along with that bag. Now I know he must have had an accomplice. This note was constructed with precision and neatness. There's not a crooked cut on one of the pasted letters. Lynch couldn't cut his own throat right. Someone else put this together. Let's find out who."

Shockey hurried toward the front of the house, intent on getting back to headquarters. He had to notify McCandless about this new twist. The LeBeau woman could still be in danger. The kidnappers might try again.

A small boy on a bicycle was riding in and out among the parked police cars, obviously lost in a game of make-believe, imitating the sound of a siren, pedaling furiously in a fantasy chase.

"Hey, kid," Shockey called. "You better get on home. This is not a safe place for you to play."

"I'm gonna be a cop when I grow up," he announced, as Shockey started to get in his car.

"That's right?" Shockey asked, and looked again at the serious expression on the skinny little kid who was watching his every move.

"Yeah!" he cried. "You got a badge? Can I see it?"

"Yeah, sure, kid," Shockey agreed, and pulled the folded piece of well-worn leather from his pocket. It wasn't often he ran across a kid who liked cops. Usually it was just the opposite. He couldn't resist doing a little public relations work.

"Boy!" the kid whispered, as he ran a dirty little finger over the shiny metal shield with Shockey's identification number on it. "I told the sheriff down the driveway I was going to be a cop, but he didn't have no badge. Not like this he didn't."

"What sheriff, son? Why did you think he was a sheriff?" Something made Shockey pursue this odd little kid's rambling story further.

"Well, he was coming up here before he nearly ran me over..." He looked up cautiously, suddenly afraid that it would come out that he hadn't looked before he darted through the thick undergrowth. But nothing was said to correct him, and so he continued his story, tracing every curve and ridge in the silver badge as he talked. "And, I knew he was a sheriff cause he had a big hat like the ones on television."

Shockey's eyes narrowed. *Nothing odd in that,* he cautioned himself. "Go on," he urged the kid.

"Well, I told him you guys was already up here, and I guess he decided to leave, cause he rolled his car window up and drove away. That's all."

"What did he look like?" Shockey persisted. Something told him if he'd arrived thirty minutes later this morning, they might all have been saved further investigation.

"I don't know. Just a cowboy. I got to go now," he said, and reluctantly handed back the badge.

Shockey watched the kid leave, pedaling furiously as he darted between two of the parked black and whites. *Cowboy? What would Wiley Lynch be doing hanging out with a cowboy?*

He set the thought aside for the time being and hurried to his car. He had to make that phone call to Tulsa.

Chapter 7

"Where's Maggie?" Jesse asked breathlessly as she dashed through the kitchen door into the house.

King looked up and tried not to glare at Jesse's exuberance. Her hair was windblown, the black and white polka-dot tank top she was wearing was half in and half out of the tightest pair of blue jeans he'd ever seen anybody wear and breathe in at the same time. And, to make matters worse, she was barefoot.

"Where are your shoes?" he shouted, and then took a deep breath along with a calming gulp of lukewarm coffee.

He'd been dawdling over breakfast for half an hour, waiting for Jesse to appear, and then she came through the door like a Texas twister. It was obvious she'd been up and about far longer than he had.

"My shoes are on the porch," she answered calmly. "They're dirty. I didn't want to track up the floor. Where's Maggie?" she repeated, refusing to let King's bad mood spoil the most perfect morning she'd had in years.

"In her room," King answered reluctantly, and felt his gut kick at the backside view of Jesse in those jeans, as she dashed through the kitchen toward Maggie's private rooms.

Jesse knocked once and then let herself in as she called out, "It's me."

"Come in, sweetheart," Maggie answered, as she came from the bathroom where she'd obviously been putting the finishing touches on hair and make-up. Her short, ample figure was corseted and bound with determination. Her long, gray braid was set higher on her head than usual, and her little round face was lightly decorated with blush and lipstick. She looked like an aging cherub. She also looked adorable.

Today was Friday. It was double coupon day at her favorite supermarket and she had a grocery list a mile long.

"Would you mind picking up my birth control pills?" Jesse asked, as she pulled a piece of paper from the pocket of her shirt. She'd been using them for years to correct a very painful and irregular period. "I called my doctor in St. Louis yesterday. He said he'd call in a prescription at this pharmacy." She handed the paper to Maggie.

"You still have to take these?" Maggie asked, and

looked sharply at the expression on Jesse's face. She'd always known about Jesse's problem. She'd hoped time would correct it. Obviously it had not.

"Yep," Jesse grinned, leaned over and kissed Maggie's frown. "But don't worry. They haven't made a scarlet woman of me yet."

Jesse laughed at the horrified expression on Maggie's face, and then suddenly they were both chuckling loudly.

King heard the laughter and felt an awful tinge of jealousy. He couldn't make Jesse laugh. He hadn't even been able to make her smile since they'd come home. If anything, he'd only made matters worse. He was tired, miserable, and worried, and knew he couldn't take many more nights like last night. He hadn't slept a wink, knowing Jesse was across the hall. He'd thought all night long of Jesse and her statement that Duncan had come to visit her in St. Louis. He just couldn't get past the thoughts that jeered at his conscience during the long hours until dawn. Why did he care who went to see Jesse? He had made no effort to be one of the visitors. He had simply let time and Jesse slip through his fingers. He heard the women coming from Maggie's room, and yanked a piece of newspaper up in front of him.

Maggie rummaged through her purse, checking for all the necessary lists and coupons, then waved a casual goodbye in Jesse's direction before hurrying out the door. It was obvious Maggie was going to make a day of her trip to Tulsa.

Silence filled the kitchen, and Jesse debated with herself about trying to talk to an obviously disgruntled man. She wisely decided to keep her own counsel, and started back outside to retrieve her boots and get on with her plans for the day when something odd about King's newspaper caught her eye. Without saying a word, she walked over to King, gently peeking over the wall of newsprint he'd erected between them. Ignoring the furious glare he shot her way, she carefully took the paper, turned it over until it was right side up, handed it back, and watched with glee as a dark red flush crept up past the neck of his brown, plaid workshirt.

"Do you mind if I ride Tariq?" she asked.

King slammed the useless paper down on the kitchen table and stood with a jerk. He leaned over until they were practically nose to nose and growled.

"Looks to me like you already did."

Jesse shrugged self-consciously, knowing Tariq was King's favorite, and the one he usually chose to ride when out on the range. He was a large, white, spirited Arabian with an easy gait and Jesse preferred him to several of the smaller, more highly strung horses.

"Do you care?" she persisted, and tried to forget how angry King could get if pushed too far.

"Obviously what I think matters damn little to you. Jesse Rose. Do what you want…you always do." Then before she disappeared completely, he couldn't stop himself from grabbing her hands and turning the palms up for a careful inspection.

They looked healed. He knew they were getting stronger and stronger each day, by the amount of use she gave them, but his Arabian stallion was a big, high-spirited mount. He wasn't sure her grip was strong enough to handle him. He sighed, reluctantly dropped her hands, and looked up, unable to decipher the odd, almost expectant expression on her face.

"Be careful," he warned, and was saved from making a complete fool of himself by the phone's ring.

Jesse bolted out the door, grabbing her boots on the run.

By the time King hung up the phone and hurried toward the corrals, Jesse was long gone toward the big, shady pond more than half a mile away.

"Turner," King shouted, as he neared the corrals, new fear mixing with the old at what he'd just learned.

The phone call had been from St. Louis. King still had trouble assimilating Shockey's news. Kidnap Jesse? What in the world would someone hope to gain? She wasn't *that* wealthy. Almost everything she'd inherited was invested in a way that would take months, even years, to liquidate. She didn't *have* half a million dollars. And she had no family. Who would a kidnapper think was going to pay the ransom?

Then King stopped. He turned slowly as a terrible possibility entered his mind. He looked around at the land with new vision—McCandless land that went for miles and miles, the more than comfortable ranch house, the millions of dollars invested in the Arabians, the cattle, oil interests—and he knew who the kidnappers had targeted. It was King that would have come up with the money, and easily enough at that. The kidnappers had to know he would give everything he owned if it meant Jesse's well-being.

King shuddered, wiped a shaky hand across his eyes, and swallowed hard, pushing back the nausea that boiled inside him. Jesse was to have been the victim, but it was King's ransom they were after.

"Turner!" he called again, and breathed a sigh of relief as the older man came hobbling through the doorway of the hay barn. Turner waved at King, indicating his whereabouts.

"In here," he called, and waited as King came running.

"Jesse," he asked quickly. "Where?"

"Didn't say," Turner replied, and then frowned at the worried expression on his boss's face. "What's wrong?" he asked. "She'll be okay. That horse loves her...always did. He ain't gonna hurt Jesse."

"The police," King muttered, pointing toward the house.

He was back in McCandless shorthand, but Wil Turner was more than used to it. This was the second generation of McCandless he'd worked for.

"What about the police?" he asked, and led the way back inside, out of the hot sun and wind.

"Just called. Wasn't attempted murder. Jesse stopped a kidnap attempt. They also didn't get the sonofabitch. He's still out there."

"Well, I'll be," Turner muttered. "This does put a

different light on things, don't it, boy? Well, now. I'm sure she can go for a horse ride here on the ranch and come to no outside harm.''

King started to argue, but Turner's slow drawl and common sense were beginning to calm the fear and rage boiling inside.

"King," Turner continued. "Jesse went that direction." He pointed toward the hills, away from the roads and ranch house. "And the only way to get to Jesse there is to come through here. That is unless they come by helicopter, and it don't sound to me like them kidnappers is that smart. Just look what one little girl did to their plans. What do you say?" He waited for King's reply, and then added with a rueful pat on King's back, "I'll send one of the boys after her right now, if you think best. I know what she means to you…to all of us. But I also know how bad this has been on her. First time I seen her really smile since she's been here was this morning when she got on that horse."

King paced between Turner and the barn door several times before jamming his hands in his pockets in frustration.

"Let her ride," he finally agreed. "But if she's not back by noon, we're going after her."

"You got it, boss," Turner agreed, and wisely went back to work.

The sun was bright, almost white in the faded blue sky. Not one puny cloud dared to show face in the building heat. The dry, brown grass broke and scattered like dust as King's big stallion ran at an easy gallop. His nostrils flared, and his ears twitched at the sounds coming from his rider. He didn't know what laughter was, but he responded to Jesse's joy and pleasure. He tossed his head and nickered at a herd of Black Angus cattle trying to graze on the brittle pasture land.

Jesse felt the stallion's power beneath her, but knew no fear. He was nothing she couldn't handle. She trusted Tariq completely. King had trained him well.

"We're almost there, boy," Jesse said to the horse, and watched his ears twitch at the sound of her voice.

She knew when the horse smelled the water. His stride lengthened and he strained at the resistance of Jesse's grip on the reins. She didn't dare let Tariq have his head. Her hands weren't strong enough to hold on, or even stop him, if he was allowed to run at full gallop.

Finally they topped the gently rolling hill above the pond and stopped. Jesse let Tariq run the short distance to the water's edge where the bits of tender green grass still grew in sparse abandon. She dismounted and let the reins trail the ground without tying Tariq, knowing King trained his horses to stand in this manner. The big horse blew softly through his velvety nostrils, tossed his head, and then began to graze slowly along the edge of the pond and down the gentle slope of the dam.

Jesse didn't hesitate any longer. Looking around carefully just to assure herself that she was truly alone, she kicked off her boots and began to peel away her sweaty clothes, layer by layer.

The water was cooler than expected. She grimaced as a wave lapped at the calves of her legs, then slipped up past her thighs as she waded deeper. Finally she leaned forward and slipped silently into the inviting depths.

It was heaven. Jesse knew from past experience that absolutely nothing was as exhilarating as a skinny dip on a hot, summer day. She swam. She floated. She waded at waist deep level until the skin on her back began to draw and tingle. Jesse knew she'd probably stayed too long and would have a good sunburn, but it had been worth it.

She reluctantly waded from the water and dabbed at the quickly drying moisture on her bare body with the tail of her shirt. Once out of the water, Jesse felt compelled to hurry. She'd just pulled on her last boot and was trying in vain to run a comb through the wet tangles in her hair when she heard a loud commotion begin over the next hill.

She whistled for the horse, and breathed a sigh of relief as he quickly answered her call. He came at a trot, also disturbed by the noise coming from over the hill. He pranced sideways as Jesse tried to mount. She spoke sharply and yanked on the reins, bringing Tariq back into position, then swiftly mounted. The closer she rode toward the sounds, the more certain she knew what she would see when topping the hill.

Sure enough, something was after King's two-year-olds, and Jesse quickly spotted the trouble as the herd separated, running wildly away from a pack of dogs chasing at their heels. Jesse watched in frustration, unsure of what to do first, when one horse went to his knees. She gasped and started forward when the horse recovered as quickly as he'd fallen and continued his flight to safety.

She breathed a sigh of relief and decided to turn Tariq toward the ranch to go for help when a series of events took the decision out of her hands.

One of the young horses was cut off from the others with knife-sharp precision, the same way a pack of wolves would cut off their prey from a herd before closing in for the kill. The horse ran full tilt through some scrub brush, and plunged headlong in wild flight into a small pond used for watering the stock. Jesse saw the floating plastic milk jugs spaced out across one end of the pond just before the horse plunged headfirst among them. She knew instantly that someone's trespassing onto King's property was going to cause great harm.

"Oh, no!" she whispered, and leaned over Tariq's massive neck, clutching at his long, wiry mane. She saw the horse below begin to thrash wildly about in the water, unable to run any farther, unable to move. He'd been caught in a trot-line—a long fishing line that Turner called a lazy man's way to fish.

The line usually ran the length of a pond, or across the neck, and had large, barbed hooks set at spaced intervals and at certain depths, angling for the big ones that rested along the pond bottoms when weather was hot and dry. The jugs were used as floats and markers, so that the fisherman could pole a boat along and check each jug to see if the hook dangling below had catch waiting to be harvested.

Jesse knew that if she went back to the ranch, it would be too late to help the horse. The dogs would have killed it before any help could possibly arrive. Without thought for her own dangers, she urged Tariq down the hill. Her screams and shouts and the stallion's wild race toward them halted the dogs. They scattered, tails between their legs.

"Now what?" she asked herself, as she quickly dismounted and looked about, hoping the dogs had headed for easier game. "Okay," she said, talking aloud in an effort to calm the trapped and frightened horse. "It's just you and me, boy."

She took the rifle from the scabbard behind the saddle, wrapped the reins firmly around the saddle horn, knowing Tariq would run as long as they stayed in place, and slapped him sharply on the rump. She watched the big horse disappear over the hill, racing back toward the ranch, and hoped she'd done the right thing. She knew the quickest way to get help was to send Tariq home alone. She also knew it would probably scare King to death, but she felt she had no choice.

She checked the rifle, making certain that it was loaded, pumped a shell into the chamber and then took it off safety. She'd be ready if the dogs came back. She just hoped to God they didn't. She was a terrible shot.

"Okay, pretty boy," Jesse said in a low, calm voice and stepped slowly into the water. The water came over the tops of her boots, slowly seeping down inside as she waded toward the trapped horse. But she soon had to stop as her progress agitated the horse further. She had no choice but to stand knee-deep in the muddy water, waiting between the frightened animal and whatever came into her gun sights. Help had to come soon.

"Sweet Jesus!" Turner said under his breath, as he saw Tariq come racing down the hill toward the ranch. "King!" he shouted at the top of his voice, and ran to open the corral gate.

King had started to the house when he heard his foreman's frantic call. What he saw sent him back to the barns with a prayer in his heart and on his lips.

"She's been at the pond for sure," Turner said, pulling a bit of green grass caught in Tariq's bridle.

King nodded, yelled for two of the men to follow in the ranch truck, and headed for his horse. He grabbed the reins from Turner's hands and swung into the saddle. His feet never touched the stirrups as his long legs scissored the air. Dust boiled and grass flew from beneath the stallion's hooves as King turned him toward the pond and gave him his head.

He squinted his eyes against the blinding glare of the sun and dust flying through the air in the hot summer wind. Tariq's great speed and endurance proved itself worthy. He made it back to the pond in record time.

King pulled back sharply on the reins and felt the big horse sawing the bit back and forth in his mouth as he fought King for domination. King persisted, and the big stallion finally came to a halt under a withering blackjack tree beneath the pond dam.

He searched the entire area frantically, unable to see any sign of Jesse. His heartbeat was as erratic as Tariq's behavior, and his breath came in sharp, choking gasps. He wanted to scream Jesse's name aloud, but couldn't find the air in his lungs to do so. Just as he caught his breath enough to call out, a gunshot echoed through the meadow. Tariq jumped nervously beneath him. Only the powerful grip of King's legs kept the horse from bucking him off. King spun the horse around in the general direction of the shot and kicked Tariq in the flanks. The great horse needed no further urging as he rapidly climbed the hill's steep incline.

"Somebody better hurry," Jesse muttered aloud, and tried to mask her panic as the dog pack reappeared on the crest of a hill above the small pond.

The dogs saw her and stopped, barked several times, but didn't move from their position.

Jesse knew it would only be a matter of time before they got up the nerve and try another run. Desperation and hunger made vicious animals out of man's best friends. These weren't naturally wild animals. They had once been someone's family pets. But they'd been dumped; abandoned by those they had trusted. Now they only had themselves to depend on. Unfortunately for Jesse, these kinds of animals had less fear of humans than a wolf or coyote would have, and Jesse knew she might not be able to stop their charge.

The young horse snorted wildly, also sensing the dogs reappearance, and thrashed weakly, still frantically trying to free himself from the heavy nylon line and sharp hooks. But his movement only drove the hooks deeper and wrapped the line tighter. Finally, he stopped, trembling with shock and pain. Jesse's low, easy crooning broke through his panic, and he turned pain-filled brown eyes her way.

"Whoa, boy," Jesse whispered softly, and held out her hand, letting the horse smell her, touch her outstretched fingers with the soft pelt of his nose. She just wanted to let him know she was still here. "It's gonna be okay, pretty fellow," she said softly, knowing the sound of her voice was somewhat calming to the animal. "King will come and he'll take good care of you...yes, he will." She couldn't stop the tears that came to her eyes as she continued. "He took care of me. He'll take good care of you, too."

Jesse winced as the sun beamed down on her already burning skin. She dipped her hand into the water, cupped it, and carried a handful to her hot, sweaty face, sighing with short-lived relief as she splashed the overheated areas with the muddy water. It dried almost instantly in the intense noon-day sun.

She shifted the gun to a different position. Her hands were cramping and aching, unused to gripping anything as tightly as she was holding the rifle. But she didn't flinch. She kept her gaze on the dog pack lining the hilltop.

Nearly twenty minutes passed with no movement from the dogs, and Jesse looked frantically down at her watch, shaking it to make certain it still worked. The watch was running all right, and so were the dogs as they came down the crest of the hill.

Jesse's heart stopped. Then she took a breath, glad the other horses were completely over on the other side of the meadow. She took aim. She knew if the horses had been anywhere close, she'd just as likely hit one of them as a dog. Suddenly she wished she'd paid more attention to Andrew McCandless's instructions, but it was too late now. The dogs were closer, running with an ominous silence, intent on one goal. Food! Woe be to anything, or anyone, who got in their way.

Jesse could hear the horse behind her begin to thrash around in the water. He, too, sensed impending doom, but she couldn't worry about that now.

She took a deep breath, shaky aim, and fired at the big shepherd dog in front of the pack, then pumped another shell into the chamber.

King took one swift look at the scene before him, reached behind his saddle for the rifle that was usually within hand's reach and then groaned. Jesse had it. With little urging, Tariq retraced his steps, and flew into the confusion below with wild abandon.

Jesse heard the hammer of horse hooves coming down the hill behind her, and prayed it was help arriving, because she'd missed her shot. She watched in fright as the dogs regrouped for another run. She heard King call her name, and turned with relief as he dismounted on the run and jumped into the water with both feet. His only goal was to reach Jesse before the dogs did.

King snatched the rifle from her hands, shooting three times in quick succession. A sharp yelp of pain sent the dogs running back up the hill, and King managed to hit two more and wound another before they disappeared.

He watched them run out of rifle range and knew how closely he'd come to arriving too late. He turned silently, took one long look at Jesse standing wet and bedraggled, threw the rifle onto the edge of the grass, and pulled her into his arms without saying a word.

She felt him shudder, and heard him swallow several times before he pulled back and tried to speak.

Jesse knew he was angry with her because his dark eyes literally took her apart at the seams. He kept running his hands carefully over her body, up and down her arms several times, as if assuring himself she was still in one piece.

He wasn't going to be able to stop the quick tears of relief that gathered in the corners of his eyes, but didn't care if Jesse saw them or not. He'd been too frightened to have time to get mad. Then when Jesse hugged him he couldn't have worked up a good mad if he'd tried.

Jesse sighed wearily and leaned into him, too tired

and worn out to worry about him getting the wrong notion.

"What took you so long?" she asked, trying to lighten the situation between them.

King cupped her face in his hands. His thumbs lightly traced the sensual fullness of her lower lip, as he let himself absorb the fact that Jesse was truly safe. He felt the intensity of heat radiating from the skin beneath his fingers and sighed. What he was about to do would probably set their relationship back even further, but he couldn't help himself. He leaned closer, felt Jesse stiffen beneath his touch, and saw her lips opening. She never got the opportunity to voice her thoughts. King took her breath and thoughts away as he pulled her out of the water, off her feet, and into his arms.

He felt hot and cold at the same time, as the taste of Jesse's lips sent his sanity begging. He'd known, somewhere in the back of his mind, that this would happen—that touching her would be all fire, demanding and consuming, as she answered the pressure of his kiss with a claim of her own. He couldn't think past the softness of her mouth and the tiny, almost undetectable moans that he heard every time he started to let her go. King held her against his body and felt every muscle in him swell with wanting more. He needed to lay her down on the hard, dry grassland and lose himself in Jesse's sweet warmth. But this wasn't the time, or the place, to see how far Jesse would let him venture into uncharted territory. He drew back reluctantly and stroked her lips with his fingertip, needing the reassurance that she was still within reach and touch.

"Honey, you scared me to death," he said huskily.

Jesse blinked, trying to regain a measure of her equilibrium, but the sight of that beautiful, demanding mouth, just inches away, that had nearly driven her mad, and the touch of his fingers on her lips, made the world go around and around. Finally, the soft whinny of the injured horse brought them both back to their senses.

"The horse, King! It's caught in a trot-line. I couldn't get close enough to help him."

"Horse?" he muttered, slowly coming to his senses. Then realizing what she was trying to say, he turned toward the trapped animal. A string of muffled curses fell from his lips as he saw the young horse's plight. King whistled for Tariq, got a lariat from the saddle, and quickly made a makeshift bridle for the trapped animal. Walking slowly through the water, until he reached the horse's side, he carefully placed the bridle over the horse's head and ran his hands slowly down it's neck and mane.

"Let me see what you've done to yourself, fella," King said as he worked. He handed the other end of the rope to Jesse, then carefully began to trace the course of the nylon under the water.

The horse nickered, recognizing a familiar smell and voice, and stood quietly as King's husky growl and gentle hands quickly freed him from the trap of hooks and nylon cord. Several hooks were imbedded too deeply, and King refused to touch them. Instead he cut away the cord and left them for the vet to remove. He waded the length of the pond neck, angrily pulling at the remaining rope and floats and nearly had it cleared when the ranch pickup truck topped the hill above the pond and started down the steep incline.

As soon as the driver came near enough, King called out, sending them back to the ranch to get a horse trailer for the injured animal. He wasn't about to walk the young horse back in this heat after such a trauma.

He threw the trot-line to one side of the grass to be picked up by his ranch hands, and eyed the dead animals on the opposite hillside. The men could dispose of them, too. He wasn't leaving Jesse or the horse.

She sat on the grassy edge of the pond, pulling first one boot off and then the other, pouring a stream of muddy water from each. She watched King lead the horse from the water and tie the end of rope to a piece of deadwood. This horse was too young and frightened to trust it not to run.

"Couldn't wait to take off those boots, could you?" King teased softly, trying to ease the tension growing between them. And then he frowned, becoming aware of the increasing redness on Jesse's face and neck and down her bare arms. "Looks like you took off more than shoes today, didn't you, Jesse Rose? You're gonna be sick."

Jesse looked up and smiled shyly before passing off an answer with a shrug of her shoulders, then wincing at the movement.

King muttered under his breath. He unbuckled his belt and pulled his shirt tail out of his Levi's.

Jesse's eyes widened. She managed not to stare as she sneaked delighted peaks at King's impromptu strip-tease. Then she couldn't resist adding, "If we only had a little music while you took it all off."

King's eyes narrowed. He glared as he handed her his shirt and jammed his wide-brimmed Stetson on her head. "Shut up and put this on," he ordered.

Jesse needed no further urging. She sighed with relief as she covered her burning skin.

"We have to talk," King said, "but now's not the time. I've got to get you, and the horse, back to the ranch." Then his voice deepened and the ominous tone scared Jesse to death. "There's something you need to know."

Chapter 8

King watched the veterinarian drive away from the ranch and started into the house, only to be stopped by Maggie's arrival with a carload of groceries. By the time pleasantries had been exchanged and all the groceries carried inside, half an hour had elapsed. King was worried about how to tell Jesse that the attack had been more than attempted murder. He didn't know how to tell her about the kidnap attempt without frightening her more. Maggie's advice gave him no easy way out.

"Just tell her, King," Maggie ordered, as she moved about the kitchen, putting away the day's purchases. "She's tougher than you give her credit for. And, when you go," she added, pulling a small, white stack from her purse, "give her this."

King took the sack and started toward Jesse's bedroom. He was more than halfway there before it dawned on him that he was delivering a prescription. His first thought was that Jesse was sick and hadn't told him. But the flat, round shape inside the sack could only mean one thing. Feelings went off inside him like a four-alarm fire. He'd seen those packets inside more than one woman's purse. Birth control pills! *Why is the thought so upsetting to me?* he wondered. He knew it was modern, wise, accepted. But he didn't like the idea of Jesse needing to be protected. That meant being exposed to the possibilities of pregnancy, and that meant a man involved with Jesse in a manner that made his blood pressure rise. By the time he got to her room and walked through the open door, he'd worked himself into a silent rage.

Jesse heard footsteps, knew they were King's, and sighed miserably, as she lay face down on her bed, as near naked as possible yet still retaining a measure of decency. There wasn't an inch of skin anywhere on her body that had escaped sunburn, and she was in no mood for a lecture about her methods of saving horses.

"Maggie said to give this to you," he growled, and slammed the sack on the pillow beside her face.

Jesse took one look at the sack and smiled to herself in spite of her misery.

"Thank you very much," she said in an off-hand manner.

"I don't even know you, do I, Jess?" King muttered, trying to ignore all the bare skin in plain view. There wasn't much to the bath towel, nor much left to the imagination. Keeping Jesse covered was proving to be vital to King's sanity.

"You never paid any attention to me before, or you'd know I've taken these since I was seventeen. They correct a very miserable medical problem that's none of your business," Jesse said sharply. She groped toward the nightstand for her sunburn lotion. "If you want to know about my current medical history, smart ass, try rubbing some of this aloe vera gel on my back. My sunburn is killing me."

King turned as red as Jesse's back and was glad she couldn't see his face. He yanked the tube of lotion from her hands and sat down on the side of the bed, trying to ignore Jesse's body. He was more disturbed by what was not visible than by all the bare skin he *could* see, and hesitated momentarily before he unscrewed the cap on the tube of lotion. The gel was a cool, clear green as King squeezed it into the palm of his hand. But it quickly liquified into a clear film on Jesse's hot skin.

"Oooh," Jesse sighed with relief, as the aloe quickly took away the miserable burning sensation. "That feels wonderful," she mumbled into her pillow. King smiled to himself and continued to apply the gel with long, gentle strokes.

"I should have remembered. You have a great set of hands," Jesse teased, and grinned into her pillow as she felt his hands instantly cease movement on her body.

King practically vaulted from the bed, slapping the plastic tube back on the nightstand within Jesse's reach.

"Damn you, Jesse," he muttered. "One of these days you'll push me a little too far."

King was furious with himself as well as with Jesse. He let her bait him and then fell neatly into every pothole of the conversation with his usual lack of grace.

It had been difficult enough having to touch her in such an intimate manner, knowing full well that he wasn't going to do a thing about it. It didn't do his blood pressure any good to know Jesse was as aware of it as he was.

"I need to talk to you," he said, pacing the floor by her bed, nervously trying to sort out his thoughts.

"Look," Jesse began. "I'm sorry I took a chance you didn't approve…"

"No," he interrupted. "It's not about that. It's about the phone call I got when you left to go riding." Then he couldn't stop from adding, "And decided to play Annie Oakley instead."

"What about the phone call?" she questioned, not liking the turn of conversation, or King's tone of voice. She carefully turned to face him. The bath towel slipped and she pulled it quickly back in place as she turned, then winced as the bedclothes collided with her tender skin.

"For God's sake!" King whispered, watching in horror as the towel covered even less of her front. He grabbed a soft, cotton robe from her closet, then practically threw it at her. "You're going to have to suffer for a few minutes. I've had just about all I can take from you today, Jesse Rose."

His words were short and clipped, his voice gruff, and Jesse knew he meant it. She grabbed at the robe and shrugged into the arms, belting it loosely around her while King stood with his back to her bed.

"You can turn around now," she said, and tried not to grin. The look on his face took the laughter out of her voice.

"Shockey called," King blurted out, unable to find any easy way to say this. "They found Lynch's house. But he'd already gone."

"Great," she muttered. Frustration and disappointment overwhelmed her. She combed her hands through her hair in short jerky movements. She'd been counting on his arrest. She was so tired of being afraid.

"That's not all they found," King said, and then squatted down beside Jesse's bed, needing eye contact to finish his message. "Honey...they also found a ransom note."

Her shock was obvious; her reaction extreme. She bounded from her bed as if trying to escape from the implications that went with King's announcement.

"Ransom? Why in God's name would someone try to kidnap me? I don't have any family. I don't have money like that...do I?"

She sounded so little...and so lost. King sighed, wanting to assure her, yet knowing that the rest of what he had to say was only going to make matters worse.

"No, baby," he said. His voice became even huskier as emotion thickened his speech. "I don't think they expected you to come up with the half million."

Jesse's mouth flew open, and she sank back on the edge of the bed with a stunned expression on her face.

"Half a million...dollars?" she asked, her eyes wide with shock. "They *are* crazy. I don't have anything like that."

Jesse watched King pace before the window, jam his hands in his pockets and then turn to face her, an almost defiant expression on his face.

"I don't think you were the target, Jesse. I think I was. You were just the victim."

Jesse heard the pain in his voice and saw the guilt on his face. She realized with startling clarity that he was probably correct. But she wouldn't allow the guilt he stood ready to accept.

"None of this is your fault. No more than it's anyone's fault to be a victim of any crime. Greed is what's at fault, King. Not you. And not me."

King let out a slow, uneasy breath. Gratitude for her understanding made him feel a bit easier, yet he was uncertain if Jesse had grasped the full implication of the news. He walked over to the bed and sat down beside her. He separated her hands from their tight wad in her lap and lifted first one and then the other up to the light. They were very nearly well. All that remained was the tiny network of red lines that faded more with each passing day.

"You know what this means now, don't you?"

Jesse looked up at the expression of concern on his face and something...some other undefinable look that he kept trying to hide. She restrained from touching him, letting her eyes caress him instead.

His dark hair lay in tousled abandon. There was a piece of grass stuck in the collar of his shirt, and Jesse watched his dark eyes follow her every movement.

"Yes," she finally answered, then slowly pulled her hands away. "It means this is not over. That they could try again."

She couldn't disguise the tremble in her voice, nor the tears that sprang to her eyes. She also knew that she might not be as lucky if a next time ever came. She wanted to cry. *It wasn't fair, and it was no one's fault.*

"I think I want to be alone now," she whispered, refusing to look at the hurt and rejection she knew was on his face.

"I'll leave you for now, Jesse Rose," King whispered as he leaned over and brushed the top of her head with his lips. "But you'll never be alone. Not as long as I'm alive. Remember that."

She let the tears spill over and the sadness come as King left her room. Was this nightmare ever going to end?

Lynch was gone all right. The man slammed the phone down with a furious jerk and began to pack. Lynch had disappeared from the house. He was not in the city. He was gone from the state. His sources were good; the information solid. He had a terrible, sinking feeling that he knew where Lynch was headed.

He looked at himself in the dresser mirror, saw the peeling paint and the crack on the wall behind him, but couldn't look at the face staring back in accusation. How had he let this happen? It had gotten out of hand so quickly. All he'd wanted was what was due him. No one was to have gotten hurt. He knew he was on a downhill road, and the only thing waiting for him at the bottom was disaster…unless…unless he could find Wiley Lynch soon.

He grabbed his suitcase and headed for the door. Now there was only one place left for him to go. He had to go back, to the beginning.

"Thanks for coming," Duncan said, as he greeted King. "Come in, please. I've just returned from a short trip. The place is messy."

King frowned as he followed his uncle into the room. He hated these visits. He was always ill at ease around Duncan. And the only time he received an invitation to visit was when Duncan was short of money.

He watched with a forced lack of expression as Duncan sauntered over to a wet bar opposite the living room window and poured himself a drink. He shook his head, refusing Duncan's offer to pour him a glass.

Duncan shrugged and downed the shot of whiskey neat, fortifying himself for what lay ahead. He walked toward the window of his Tulsa high-rise apartment and looked over the skyline of the metropolis.

The apartment was the epitome of good living and

as usual, way beyond Duncan's means. But he liked to live fast and high, and this was the best way to go.

"How much do you want?" King drawled, anxious to get the meeting over with.

Duncan turned his head sharply and swallowed the angry retort that bubbled into his mouth. He supposed he deserved that.

"I don't want any money. I want to know how Jesse's doing."

Duncan's refusal of money left King speechless. That was a first! He narrowed his eyes and a muscle in his jaw clinched and jerked before he answered.

"She's fine. Recovering from a sunburn. Maggie said she told you about the ransom note." King watched a strange, dark look come and go on Duncan's face.

"Yes, she told me," Duncan answered, and then turned his back to King as he continued. "You've got to be careful. He may try again."

King watched Duncan's strange, evasive behavior, and felt a sense of confusion at everything going on around him. He'd had just about all of the odd little answers and hints he was going to take. He took a deep breath and threw his suspicions out into the room between them.

"Duncan, why is Jesse afraid of you? What's between you? She told me you visited her in St. Louis," King accused. "What the hell did you do to her?"

"Do? I didn't *do* anything. And of course I visited her. Just because she moved didn't mean she died."

Duncan was smooth. His manner was cool. He didn't know what Jesse had told King, but he doubted she'd said much. Knowing his nephew as he did, if she'd told the whole story, he would have been greeted with a punch in the nose. King was so single-minded about everything.

Duncan had learned long ago to persuade, not provoke. Still, he'd never been able to achieve the measure of success that seemed to fall into King's lap. He failed to see that King worked long and hard to earn the respect and rewards that Duncan felt were his due by virtue of birth alone. They were so alike, and yet so different.

Duncan cast a sly, sideways glance at King's stiff, defensive attitude and couldn't resist a final dig.

"Didn't you ever visit Jesse? She was very lonesome."

King looked long and hard at his uncle's bland expression. He didn't believe anything that came out of his mouth.

"I asked you a question," King whispered. "What happened in St. Louis? Why is Jesse afraid of you?"

Duncan glanced quickly at King, and saw him waiting for an answer with an expression on his face that made Duncan very nervous.

"She has nothing to be afraid of," he said quietly, and walked toward King. "Not from me...not anymore."

"What do you mean...anymore?" King asked with a husky growl, and took a step forward.

Duncan waved him angrily away, his voice rising to a shout.

"The person Jesse needs to fear is still out there. We have to make certain he doesn't get close to her again. What are you doing to protect her?" Duncan's voice was hard. His demeanor startled King. He answered with no reservations.

"She's never alone," he said. "The men have seen the video of Lynch. They have the police sketch posted in the bunk house, but Jesse doesn't know it. And I don't want her to. Please don't say anything. I don't want her to feel like she's under guard."

Duncan nodded and walked toward his front door, carrying the refilled glass of whiskey in his hand.

"Well, King, thanks for coming. I just couldn't help worrying, and I felt uncomfortable talking about it in front of Jesse. If there is anything I can do to help, don't hesitate to ask. I will do anything you need." Then a strange, sad expression filled his eyes and he took a big gulp of whiskey. "I can do anything except come up with the half million."

King tried to hide his surprise. This odd visit was coming to a very unusual end.

Duncan slapped him jovially on the back as he left.

"Catch you on the offer of a loan some other time, nephew. I'm never going to be this noble again."

The two men stared silently at each other for what seemed an eternity, each looking at a mirror image of the other and at…what might have been.

Finally King held out his hand and caught Duncan

off guard. Duncan gulped hard, swallowed a big knot of misery he'd been carrying around forever, and muttered as he and King shook hands, "See you around, boy...and take good care of Jesse."

The door shut in King's face and left him standing in the apartment hallway, feeling as if Duncan's farewell had been final.

King couldn't sleep. His conversation with Duncan kept replaying in his mind. He'd suspected something had happened between Jesse and Duncan. Now, he was convinced of it. Why wouldn't Jesse talk to him? She used to talk to him constantly about everything. The niggling truth answered his own questions. She used to talk to him, but he suspected he rarely listened. He hadn't listened. He hadn't noticed Jesse changing and growing. He'd let her grow up and away, and never realized what he'd had until it was gone. Then he hadn't known how to get it...or her...back.

"King?" Jesse's soft voice startled him. He turned over in bed. She was silhouetted in the doorway of his bedroom.

"What is it, honey?" he asked softly, but suspected he already knew the answer.

"I can't sleep," she whispered. "My sunburn hurts and I can't get Lynch's face to go away."

The catch in her voice was his undoing.

"You want to stay here for a while? The bed is big. I won't bump your sunburn, but I can't promise not to snore."

Jesse tried to stifle a sob. King's attempt to lighten her mood only made it worse.

King was out of bed in an instant. Sunburn or not, he needed to hold her, satisfy himself that she was here and safe. Twice today he had realized how close he'd come to losing Jesse. It was only this morning, but it seemed a lifetime ago, that Tariq had come tearing down the hill toward home with an empty saddle. He couldn't forget the complete and sudden sense of loss that had encompassed him. Then, after his visit to Duncan, he'd realized how far away he'd let her slide without even realizing it. He didn't know how he was going to do it, but he wanted Jesse back.

"Come here, honey," he whispered, carefully hugging her against his bare chest.

He felt every curve and pulse point of Jesse against his skin and through the lightweight fabric of his pajama bottoms.

A fierce surge of desire, so intense it made his legs shake, swept over him. He stepped away, aware that if he remained too close, Jesse would also feel his need. He knew he couldn't get back in his bed with Jesse ever again and not make love to her. There was no nobility left in him, no more restraint.

"Lie down, Jess," he growled in a husky whisper. "I'll go get your sunburn stuff. Maybe that will help a little. I can't do anything about Lynch except promise you with my life that he won't get close to you again."

"Okay," Jesse agreed, and reluctantly let him go. Sunburn or not, she'd felt his body harden and knew he felt something for her, if only lust by proximity. Then she felt ashamed. She was actually beginning to consider taking him on any terms that he'd offer.

King sat in an overstuffed arm chair by his bedroom window and watched Jesse sleep. The sunburn was making her restless, but at least she was getting some rest. King knew there was none for him. Not while Jesse lay on his bed alone. He ached with the need to curl around her, hold her against him all through the night, then make love as the first rays of sunshine came through his windows.

He wanted to watch the look of pleasure come in her eyes as he gave her all he had to give. But he didn't move...and he watched alone as the first ray of sunshine appeared, heralding another dry, hot day.

Chapter 9

The hot wind and sun were merciless. The wind teased like a woman, blowing intermittently against King's bare brown back just enough to make him pray for the next gust to hit the rivulets of moisture that ran in a steady stream into the waistband of his Levi's. But the breeze was weak, and the temperature high, and King ended the injured horse's workout much sooner than normal. He walked him to an empty stall and turned him over to one of the ranch hands to cool down and groom.

It had been nearly a week since the incident with the dog pack. The horse was virtually healed. Although Jesse and the horse seemed to have suffered no lasting effects from the episode, King still woke up in a cold sweat from the nightmares.

He took off his Stetson, slapped it sharply against his thigh to knock off the dust, and walked over to the long, metal horse trough inside the corral. The water that first gushed from the tap was hot and slightly muddy. King stood, letting it run for a moment until it cooled and cleared. Then he leaned down and let his mouth meet the heavy stream of cool well water. He sucked greedily, replacing body fluids that the extreme heat had sapped. When his thirst was quenched, he leaned down farther and let the water run full force over his head and down the back of his neck.

Jesse lay on her stomach on a loose pile of hay and watched King as he worked. She remained unnoticed from her vantage point in the open loft window and ignored a persistent horse fly that kept dive bombing her bare legs. Her sunburn had turned a nut brown. She was nicely camouflaged in the hay and knew she'd remain undetected unless she moved or called aloud. She had no intention of doing either. The view of King from the loft was too splendid to disturb.

Jesse watched the play of muscles ripple across King's bare shoulders as he worked the horse's lead. Sweat ran down his neck and onto the powerful muscles of his chest, making them shine like polished wood. His jeans were dark, splotched by the patches of perspiration that came through the fabric and molded to his long, powerful legs with damp affection. His boots were dust-coated, completely covered by the dry, dusty fog that hovered ankle high on the floor of the corral.

She knew his strength of mind, and strength of character, but it was his sheer physical strength that drew her attention today.

Years and years of long hours and hard work had honed his body to solid bone and muscle. There wasn't a soft, weak spot anywhere. The only thing soft about King McCandless was the spot in his heart reserved for Jesse. She knew it was there, but she wanted more than compassion and affection from the man below her. She wanted pure, unadulterated love and passion.

Jesse shivered, watching as King leaned down to the running water to quench his thirst. She watched his mouth open to drink greedily from the tap, remembering the last time she'd felt that mouth on her own lips, and wished she could trade places with the water. She could quench more than thirst if he'd only let her. The kiss he'd given her at the pond had not been compassionate, nor had it been affectionate. It had been, in Jesse's estimation, devastating. But King had turned off as suddenly as he'd turned on, and Jesse hadn't been able to find the switch to his emotions again.

She sighed with frustration, and watched King turn the water off, jam his hat back on his head, and disappear into the shady depths of the barn. She lay unmoving, trying to follow his path with her ears instead of her eyes. She listened closely to him issuing instructions about ranch business and then laughing aloud at something someone said in return. She couldn't hear what they said, but she could easily hear the joy and pleasure in his voice. She sighed and wondered if she'd ever be able to make him laugh like that. It seemed all he did nowadays was frown at her, or yell when he caught her barefoot.

The horsefly darted one last time at the bare space between her shirt top and the waistband of her shorts. It flew away into the sunshine when her hand swatted at it and came much too close.

King saw the top of Jesse's head just above the pile of loose hay near the loft window as he leaned down to get a drink. It startled him, and he wondered, as he quenched his thirst, how long she'd been watching him…and why? He carried on, seemingly unaware of her presence, and then walked nonchalantly into the barn. He stood at the foot of the steps leading to the loft and, when he heard no sound or movement, pulled off his boots, hung his hat on a nail by the steps, and quickly and quietly climbed into her hideaway.

It was suddenly too quiet below, and Jesse held her breath, listening…listening.

She jumped when she heard the sound of his voice right behind her, and guiltily rolled over in the hay. King was standing at her feet with a look on his face that stopped her heart. She let her gaze run from the still-damp hair, quickly past those knowing dark eyes, to the droplets of water caught in the hair on his chest. Her look lingered longer than necessary on the tight, damp Levi's that almost lovingly cupped and molded every interesting bulge and muscle, and finally stopped her perusal at his sock-clad feet.

"You cheated," she muttered. "Where are your boots?"

King had intended to tease, but the thought disappeared with the inclination when Jesse rolled over on her back and took him apart at the seams with those secretive, big blue eyes.

Her shirt caught under her and pulled tightly across her breasts, molding them in an invitation he found hard to resist. He closed his eyes for a moment, trying to block out the image before him, and knew that resistance wasn't the only thing getting hard. It was no use. This feeling for Jesse wasn't going to go away.

He knelt down, straddling her bare, tanned legs, and braced himself above her.

Jesse felt an energy between them spark to life, and heard his heartbeat stop and then pick up rhythm with her own. She started to speak, and then forgot what she was going to say as a tiny drop of moisture clinging to his thick, dark lashes finally fell, hurtling downward to land at the corner of Jesse's mouth.

King watched, fascinated, as the droplet paused. Then, as it started to slide down the delicate curve of her chin, he lowered himself to meet it and caught the droplet with his mouth.

Jesse felt his tongue along the edge of her chin. She closed her eyes as his teeth nipped at the pale, blue vein in her neck that pulsed beneath her tan. Her hands slid up the length of his arms, feeling the muscles jumping with strain. He held himself poised above her, and Jesse felt the magic between them begin to expand.

King was watching her closely, anxious for a reaction to what he'd done.

"What are you doing?" Jesse whispered.

King watched the light flare in her eyes, and felt her heartbeat pounding beneath his chest. It was moments before he could speak. He wanted more...much more...than that tiny taste of Jesse.

"I don't know, Jesse Rose," he answered huskily. "But I do know this..."

"What?" she asked, her eyes widening as she saw his head dipping closer and closer.

"I'm going to do it again."

The sun and the heat, the sound of men's voices, and the horses nickering back and forth in the stalls below disappeared in one blinding flash as King took Jesse in his arms. There was nothing...nothing but the smell, and the taste, and the touch of Jesse filling him. He shook with a need so powerful, so overwhelming, he couldn't think. All he could do was take. Take what he'd thought of, what he'd dreamed of, ever since he'd brought Jesse home.

Her body was soft beneath him, and it made him ache with bone-jarring need. Her arms slid around his waist, pulling him closer and closer into a waiting heat.

King groaned, then reluctantly pulled away. He grabbed her hands and propped himself above her, holding her hands trapped between their bodies.

Emptiness overwhelmed her. He'd done it again. He'd let her go. Tears pooled in her eyes and slipped silently out of the corners as Jesse let desolation overwhelm her. Now, he was either going to feel sorry for her or make excuses for what had just occurred. Either way, she didn't want to hear him shut her out.

"Honey," he whispered, and bent down, quickly kissing each of her hands held trapped against his chest. "I still don't know what's happening between us. But if I don't stop now, I know what will. I don't want ever to do anything to hurt you...you know that."

He watched as Jesse slowly nodded, then pulled her hands away from his grasp. He felt her fingers trace across his lips, and caught them gently with his teeth before they ventured farther.

Jesse gasped as his teeth pressed down just enough to restrain, and felt a quickening in the pit of her stomach answer the pressure of his teeth.

"King?" Jesse asked, her voice thick and heavy with emotion.

"What, baby?"

"If you stop now, will you promise me something?" she asked, and fixed him with an uncompromising stare.

"Anything," he answered, and pressed a kiss of promise on the tilt of her nose.

"Will you promise that if we do this again...the next time...you won't stop?"

"Sweet Jesus, Jesse Rose," King groaned, and rolled over in the hay, taking Jesse with him until she was sprawled full length on top of his chest and down his legs. He wrapped her in a fierce hug, and buried his face in the curve of her neck.

"Do you know what you're doing to my will power?" he asked.

"Robbing you of it, I hope," she answered, and felt the surge of his need beneath her.

A car honked in the distance and King jumped, suddenly remembering the buyer who'd promised to come by today.

"You take more than that, girl," he muttered, as he dumped her unceremoniously in the pile of hay and struggled to his feet. "I lost my memory and good sense, too."

He turned as he started down the steps, and gave Jesse a look that made her hot and cold all over.

"Jesse," he called softly.

She looked up at the banked fire in his eyes and held her breath.

"About that promise I made..."

She waited. The horn blared again, insistently disturbing the silence between them as King whispered.

"I never broke a promise to you yet, Jesse Rose. I'm not about to now. Next time, honey...next time."

King was gone. Jesse fell back into the hay and lay quietly, staring blindly at a broken spider web high above her head in the rafters. *He said "next time."* She couldn't stop the silly smile that appeared on her face anymore than the heart-wrenching thought that followed. *Now I know he wants me. But will it be love?*

Jesse sat quietly in the living room, staring blindly at the television. If she pretended to be absorbed in the program, maybe Maggie would quit casting those anxious looks her way and King would stop fidgeting.

She'd hardly touched a bite of her evening meal, pleading loss of appetite due to the heat. The excuse hadn't washed with King or Maggie, but they'd allowed it to pass unchallenged.

Jesse was angry and overwhelmed with a feeling of helplessness unlike any she'd ever known. Just when it seemed a portion of her life might be coming together, another piece would begin to unravel.

The principal of her school in St. Louis had called. It had taken him all of three minutes to destroy what was left of Jesse's world. He'd related everyone's good wishes for her safety and health in the same breath he'd told her he'd hired a substitute teacher for her classes. Just, of course, until her "problem" was solved. The police had advised him of a possible kidnap attempt at school should her case not be solved before the semester started. It hadn't taken him long to realize what he had to do for Miss LeBeau's welfare, as well as the welfare of the children. Of course, she wasn't being replaced permanently; this was only until everything was settled.

The worry Jesse had about his statement was that her problem might never be solved. Where did that leave her? Now she had a house she couldn't go back to, a job at which she wasn't welcome, and a man who had tried to kidnap her still at large. And, here she was, hiding in the very place she'd sworn never to come back to.

"Excuse me," she muttered, looking at neither King nor Maggie, as she bolted for the front door.

They watched her go, looking helplessly at each other for guidance. Finally, at Maggie's insistence, King followed her outside into the summer night.

The night sky was unusually dark, although the moon was almost full. But Jesse didn't notice the absence of stars or the accumulation of clouds slowly gathering in the south. She was too full of herself, certain that her life had taken a downward spiral she'd never be able to stop.

A chorus of bullfrogs competed with the cricket string quartet for dominance in the night symphony. Somewhere off to the west, a coyote's single yip preceded an entire choir of howls and calls that sent a shiver down Jesse's spine. They echoed the loneliness and emptiness she felt inside. She shuddered as the coyote chorus ended as abruptly as it had begun. A few fireflies fluttered in the black space above the horizon, flickering like earthbound stars and just as hard to catch.

Jesse walked out into the enveloping darkness and let it close around her, drawing her into its secrets like a moth drawn to the light. Scents assailed her senses from every direction, and Jesse knew she could have pinpointed her location at any given moment.

The honeysuckle, heavy with sweet-smelling blossom, reclined over and along the fence around the front yard and blended its tantalizing odor with the sharper, astringent tang of towering junipers. The air was still, and only the soft, gentle night sounds intruded into Jesse's thoughts. She felt anxiety slowly seeping away. She put her hands out in front of her and when they connected with a rough, grainy textured barrier, she climbed upon the top rail of the wooden fence and took a precarious seat.

The front door slammed loudly, telling her someone had followed her into the darkness. Probably King. Her suspicions were correct and she heard his voice call out to her.

"Here," she answered, then heard him coming her way.

"What, Jesse?" King asked with his usual abbreviated speech.

"Everything is out of control," she finally answered. Her voice was barely above a whisper. She was afraid to say it too loud. What was left of her world might come apart, too.

King didn't respond, but stood silently, allowing her time to collect her thoughts before she continued.

"As of today, I no longer have a job." Then she added, "At least until this is over, which may be never. I have a house I can't go back to. I have nothing."

"Yes, you do," King answered in his deep, husky growl. "You have Maggie...and Turner...and me." Then he grudgingly added, "Hell, you even have Duncan worrying about you, and I've never known him to care about anything but himself."

He heard her sharp, indrawn breath and then nothing. No answer, no response at all to the mention of Duncan's name. King had finally had enough of this silence.

"That does it," he mumbled.

He walked so close to Jesse she could hear him breathing, yet she could barely distinguish the outline of his shoulders in the darkness.

"Jesse, I want to know...and don't lie to me. I'll know if you do. What's between you and Duncan?"

For the longest time Jesse held her silence and then, finally, she let out a long, defeated sigh, and shifted to a less precarious position on the fence.

"Nothing," she answered quietly, and then added, "at least not now."

King's heart skipped a beat. He wasn't so sure he wanted to hear the rest of her answer, but something made him persist.

"Sometimes you seem to be afraid of him. Has he...has he hurt you, or done something that made you uneasy? If he did..."

"No! No!" Jesse interrupted. "It's just, he wanted more from me than I was willing to give."

"Like what?" King asked harshly, imagining the worst. But Jesse's answer rendered him speechless.

"He wanted to marry me."

"My God!" King finally muttered. "Where the hell was I when all this was going on?" But he knew the answer to his own question before he'd finished asking it. This had all taken place after Jesse went to St. Louis.

"Do you love him?" King finally managed to ask, and felt his stomach begin to draw when she hesitated.

"No. But once, for about five minutes, I considered trying," Jesse answered sadly.

"Were you that lonely, Jess?" King muttered. "Why would you *try* to love?"

It was the longest time before Jesse spoke. She debated with herself about even answering him and then decided it was time he knew.

"I suppose…because he looked like you."

King couldn't think. He couldn't speak. He couldn't have taken a step if his life depended on it. Finally, he managed to speak past the huge, aching knot in his throat.

"Why, if he looked like me, couldn't you love him?"

Her answer nearly broke his heart.

"Because he wasn't you."

King was devastated. Everything about her demeanor told him that he'd just lost something very precious without even knowing it had been there for the taking. It hurt to think. It hurt to talk. But he had to know.

"Jesse, am I the reason you left the Double M three years ago?"

"Yes," she answered sharply. She was angry with herself for being so weak where he was concerned. Angry because King was so blind where she was concerned. "And now, it looks like you're the reason I had to come home, doesn't it? Makes you wonder just how cruel life can be with the little jokes it plays on us from time to time."

She took a deep, shaky breath and then continued.

"Just don't expect me to thank you for making me tell you what you should have known, King McCandless. It's obvious the level of caring between us is not a balanced proposition. Just as soon as this nightmare is over, and I have to believe it soon will be, I'll be out of your life. Everything will be back to normal. So please," she said with a muffled sob, "don't let my presence put any pressure on you. I don't expect anything from you...or Duncan. I've had just about all I can take from McCandless men to last me a lifetime."

She slipped off the fence rail and went past him so quietly he didn't even realize she was gone. Not until he reached out did he discover that there was nothing in his arms but empty darkness.

The clouds belched a long, low, faraway rumble. King looked up at the dark, moonless sky in surprise. Maybe it was finally going to rain. He knew the thunder was far away and moving in the wrong direction to help this dry, dusty land tonight. He also knew it would take more than rain to put his relationship with Jesse back together. He wanted to follow her into the house, finish what they'd started in the hayloft and fill the huge, aching hole she'd just punched in his heart. But now, because he'd been so blind, and made her tell more than she'd obviously intended, she'd resent anything he said or did. She was going to think it was pity, or assuaging the guilt he'd already admitted he felt because of the attempted kidnapping. They hurt her to get to him. Then he'd hurt her by being so damn

blind. Jesse was right. The McCandless men had really
let her down.

"Dear Lord," King whispered to the starless sky,
"help me find a way to make Jesse believe. I can't let
her go again. If I do, I'll lose her for sure this
time…and I think it would kill me."

He bowed his head and turned, walking back into
the house to shut out the night, and to shut himself in
with loneliness and pain.

Chapter 10

The wind whipped over the rolling hills, flattening the dry grass and weeds to the ground. It whipped Jesse's hair into her mouth and eyes with stinging gusts. She covered her mouth and nose to keep from inhaling the clouds of red dust that hurtled wildly through the air.

"Hurry!" Maggie urged, as she and Jesse grabbed at the last of the clothes on the clothesline.

Jesse nodded, waved Maggie into the house, and gathered the last of the clothes alone. The duststorm had come up so quickly. One minute the sky had been bright, the sunshine getting ready to do its worst; the next thing they realize, a low hanging pall of rusty sky was hurtling at them in gale force.

"My word!" Maggie gasped, as Jesse staggered into the door with her arms full of dusty clothes that would have to be re-washed. "This reminds me of the Dust Bowl days. Lord knows we don't want that to happen again. We sure need a rain."

"Here, Maggie," Jesse urged. "Let me start the washing. You've already done this once. This time it's my turn."

"You just talked me into it, honey. Thanks a bunch. I believe I'll go clean up while you start the wash. I feel like I just ate a bowl of sand."

Jesse grinned. "I know what you mean. Oh!" she added, "as soon as I start a load to wash, I'm going to go check on Tariq. He was out in the coral earlier this morning. I may need to put him up if someone didn't already think of it. King took most of the men with him to the stockyards. They're hauling off the herd of cattle that was pastured by the big pond."

"Okay, but be careful," Maggie cautioned, then went through the utility room into the kitchen.

Jesse put on a long-sleeved shirt to use as a shield against the sharp, stinging sand, wrapped a scarf around her head, leaving only her eyes visible, and started toward the horse barn in her makeshift armor.

The wind blew in one long, continuous blast from the Oklahoma corridor, south toward Texas, carrying dust from as far away as the Dakotas, picking up momentum and density as it passed from state to state along the line of the storm front.

Jesse struggled to keep her feet on the ground as she lowered her head and pushed herself forward step by step. She heard King's big white stallion neighing frantically as she neared the barns. The wild winds and swirling dust were driving the horse into a frenzy. There was no place he could go to get away from the storm.

Jesse dashed quickly through the barn and into the stall area leading into the corrals. She whistled sharply, but the wind blew the sound away from Tariq. He didn't hear her approach. Jesse grabbed a rope, quickly made a noose, and walked out into the corral, letting the long loop drag in the swirling dust. She didn't want to scare the horse anymore than he already was.

"Come here, boy," she called again, and this time Tariq saw her. He answered her call with a frightened nicker, spun about before he oriented himself in the storm, and came toward her at a trot.

Jesse slipped the rope over his head and quickly led him out of the storm into the shelter of the barn.

"Here's an empty stall, fella. I know you don't like to be shut up, but something tells me you won't fuss much today."

Tariq flicked his little ears back and forth, calming at the sound of Jesse's voice and the relief of being away from the stinging dust and wind. He tossed his head as she slipped the rope from his neck, then nudged her arm as she began to rub him down, brushing most of the red dirt from the horse's snowy coat.

She gave him a final pat, walked out of the stall, and shut the half door behind her. The lariat rope lay in a tangle on the barn floor and she picked it up, deftly working it into a proper nest of loops, and hung it on a peg by the stall door. She dusted her hands against her pant legs, and surprised herself when she realized all that she'd just accomplished had been done with no pain or weakness to her hands. She pulled the scarf away from her face and looked down in surprise.

"They don't hurt," Jesse whispered to herself. "My God! They don't hurt at all. Now," she muttered, pulling the scarf back around her face before making a dash for the house, "if only the rest of my life would heal as quickly."

Jesse was heartsick at the growing gap between herself and King. For the last three days he'd purposely absented himself from her presence. When he couldn't avoid her, there was a look of pain and guilt so imbedded in his eyes that Jesse didn't know how to put things right.

She didn't know whether she'd embarrassed him by her declaration, or whether all he felt was guilt at not being able to reciprocate her feelings.

This is what she'd most feared would happen if King realized she loved him. Now he was probably lost to her for good...even as a friend.

Her heart twisted in pain. She stifled the urge to cry and headed for the house.

"Wow!" Jesse gasped, as she blew through the door. "That wind is furious." She shrugged out of her scarf and jacket, tried unsuccessfully to smooth her dark tangles into some semblance of order, and staggered into King's outstretched arms. The wind outside was not as furious as King.

"What do you think you were doing?" he asked slowly, his dark eyes flashing, his mouth grim with anger.

"Putting up *your* horse," Jesse answered, trying to pull away from King's angry grasp before he could finish his urge to shake her.

"Jesse, am I ever going to be able to trust you *not* to get into trouble when I'm gone? You could have been hurt," he muttered, raking her slight figure with a frantic sweep of his eyes.

"You're what's hurting me," Jesse muttered, and watched in dismay as King's face blanched. She wished she could take back her angry taunt. But it was too late. The damage was done.

King looked blankly down at the fierce grip he had on her arms, and instantly set her free. He turned away, hunched his shoulders and leaned his head against the pane of glass in the kitchen door.

"I'm sorry," he said, clinching his hands into fists of frustration. "I'm sorry, so sorry, Jesse Rose. All I seem to be able to do is hurt you."

He felt a dark, ugly rage building; he felt himself becoming as out of control as the wind outside, and angrily drew back his fist, unconsciously aiming for the window.

Jesse acted on instinct. She caught his fist just before it connected with the glass in the door and hung on to his arm with all her might.

"No!" she cried out. "No, King. Stop it! Stop it now!"

King took a harsh, deep breath and blinked. He looked down at the dust streaks on Jesse's face, the distress filling her wide, blue eyes, and the grip she had on his arm. What the hell was wrong with him? He hadn't lost control of his emotions like this since he was a teenager.

The look on his face was so lost Jesse couldn't help herself. She stepped forward, wrapping her arms around his waist as she laid her head against his chest. His heartbeat was ricocheting against her eardrum, but the longer Jesse held him, the steadier it became. Finally, Jesse felt his arms slip around her shoulders as King relaxed and buried his face in her hair.

"I need you to forgive me, Jesse Rose," he whispered. "I need back in your life…anyway you'll have me. Please…"

Jesse's heart jumped. He finished his plea so softly she had to hold her breath to listen.

"Give me a chance, Jesse. I can't make it without you. I don't even want to try."

Jesse started to answer him, the joy in her heart spreading swiftly to her lips, when Maggie's sharp call of concern brought them both crashing down to reality.

"King, come quick!" Maggie called from the living room where she'd gone to watch television before starting the noon meal.

King and Jesse entered simultaneously, and each saw her concern. There were no words to describe the coming horror.

Easily visible through the floor to ceiling picture

window was a massive wall of smoke billowing alone in the aftermath of the subsiding dust storm. A prairie fire! And it looked as if it were heading with great speed toward the ranch adjoining the McCandless property. If they didn't get the fire under control soon, the Double M would be right in its path.

"Call county fire," King ordered. "I'll take most of the men with me. Turner and Charlie will stay here. They'll need to be ready if we don't get the fire stopped in time."

He cast a regretful glance back at Jesse, saw the worry and fear on her face, and couldn't resist. He pulled her into his arms, ignoring the look of pleased surprise on Maggie's face, and kissed her soundly.

"I'm not through with you, girl. I've got to go…and for Pete's sake…and mine," he added, "be careful."

Jesse's spirits soared along with a bright red flush on her cheeks at the look of surprise and satisfaction on Maggie's face.

"Well now," she chuckled. "I guess grass fires aren't all that's out of control around here. Come on, honey. Let's call the fire department quickly before the whole world goes up in smoke."

Time passed slowly. Jesse watched from the verandah as the county fire trucks went flying down the road in front of the ranch in a cloud of dust, followed by the volunteer fire-fighters in their personal vehicles. From time to time, Maggie would step outside and stand beside Jesse's stiff little figure, waiting sentinel on the porch steps.

"He's going to be just fine, girl," Maggie said, and slipped a comforting arm around Jesse's shoulders. "He's been doing this all of his life. Every year it's the same thing. You know that. Some fool is bound to throw a cigarette from a passing car, or decide to burn trash, even on a day like this. Then all the good men, like King, take time out to help each other. They fight fire. They fight until the fire runs out of something to burn, or they put it out, whichever comes first."

"I know," Jesse said. "But this time it's different."

"No, honey," Maggie offered. "This time you and King are what's different. When did all this happen?"

"For me," Jesse answered, "when I was sixteen, maybe seventeen. One day I looked at him, and he'd changed, or my perception of him had. Whatever. I waited and I waited for him to notice me. I wanted him to see me as an adult, but he didn't."

The break in her voice made Maggie feel guilty. She'd never suspected. Then something else occurred to her.

"Is that why you left us so suddenly?"

Jesse nodded.

"Well, it's obvious King finally noticed something," Maggie teased. "I haven't seen a kiss like that since…since…well, at least since my soap opera yesterday afternoon."

Jesse turned around and burst out laughing at Maggie's words.

The ringing telephone called Maggie indoors and it

wasn't long before she stuck her head back outside long enough to reply.

"I have to go to the Winslow place. The fire started on their property and Sue burned her hands trying to put it out. Her baby's not quite two and her husband is gone. I told her I'd help out and spend the night until her husband gets home tomorrow."

"Of course," Jesse agreed, knowing how helpless she'd been when unable to use her hands. And she'd had no one but herself to worry about. "Need a ride?" she added.

"No. One of the neighbors volunteered to come get me. You'll be all right, won't you?" Maggie asked, suddenly realizing the predicament in which she'd be leaving Jesse. They hadn't been leaving her alone. Maggie started to go back in and change her plans when she remembered. "Turner and Charlie are still here, aren't they? And King and the other men should be home before dark."

"I'll be fine," Jesse urged. "Go pack your nightie. I'll watch for your ride."

All too soon Maggie was gone. Jesse watched as the pickup truck disappeared down the driveway in a cloud of blowing dust. She looked behind her at the big, empty house, and back at the ever present clouds of smoke on the horizon. She couldn't control the shiver of fear that swept over her. *Please God, let King be safe.*

Turner and Charlie waved at her as they came around the driveway from the machine sheds, pulling a wide plow behind one of the tractors. Jesse knew they were going to make a firebreak by cutting through the thick prairie grass with the steel plowshares, turning the fire fodder under, and the clods of dry, Oklahoma soil up to the sky.

The phone rang again, and Jesse dashed to answer. It was King.

"Jesse," he asked in a rush, obviously out of breath. "Are you and Maggie okay?"

"Yes," she answered, then added, "Maggie's not here. Someone came to get her. Sue Winslow hurt herself and needed help with the baby."

"Okay, honey," he said, and then coughed.

Jesse knew he'd just turned his head away from the phone. His voice was so dry and husky she could barely understand him. She feared he'd inhaled a lot of heat and smoke.

"Are you okay?" she asked.

"I'm fine. But I need you to give Turner a message."

Jesse started to tell him Turner wasn't there either, but something made her stop.

"You need to tell him to go get the two-year-olds. You remember, Jess? The ones the dogs chased? If this fire jumps Salt Creek, they'll be in danger. Will you do that, honey?"

"Yes, I'll tend to it, King," she hedged, and knew he'd heard her hesitancy.

"Jesse, are you going to do what I asked you to do?" he growled.

"Turner's not here, King. He and Charlie are plowing a fire break," she said, her words spilling out in a rush. "I can take Tariq and go let the horses out before I can ever get Turner back to the ranch."

"No!" he shouted into the phone. "No, dammit! No, Jesse! Promise me. Don't you dare go after those horses!"

"King, if I don't, they could be trapped. Then you'd lose everything," Jesse argued.

"Jesse Rose," he shouted, and she had to hold the phone away from her ear. "I said don't go!"

But the line went dead in his ear and King threw the phone down in panic. Damn her to hell and back, she would go. He knew it. He ran past the stunned patrons of the corner quick-stop where he'd gone to use the phone, and jumped back into the borrowed Jeep. He would never get back to the Double M in time to stop her. And Jesse was wrong. He wouldn't lose a thing unless something happened to her. *Then* he'd lose everything.

The big stallion was uneasy. He danced sideways when Jesse dismounted to open the wide, wooden gate that separated the meadow above the ranch from the grass land where the horses were pastured.

She could smell smoke in the air, and if she looked closely between the trees in the distance, she could see the first hints of grayish-brown wisps gathering above the treetops.

The wind was blowing against her left cheek as she

mounted Tariq and turned him full face into the wind.
She didn't think the fire had crossed the creek yet, and
prayed the fire-fighters would be able to stop the blaze
before it did. If they could, the Double M would be
spared. But Jesse knew time was of the essence, and
kicked Tariq in the flanks, urging him at a gallop toward the big pond and the herd of two-year-olds.

She rode Tariq hard, but his seat was easy as he ran.
Jesse had no problems staying mounted. Nothing could
have prepared her for the panic and terror that lay waiting just over the hill.

The closer she got, the sharper was the tang of acrid
smoke filling the air. Jesse's heartbeat accelerated.
Smoke was blowing in long, stringy clouds, making
her eyes water and her nose burn as she reluctantly
inhaled the burning wind. Tariq tossed his head and
Jesse knew he, too, was suffering from the effects of
the fire. She leaned over in the saddle and urged him
on, knowing the horse's instincts were telling him he
was going the wrong way.

"Come on, big fellow," Jesse called in his ear.
"We're almost there."

It was after they topped the last hill above the pond
where Jesse had enjoyed her skinny dip that she saw
the extent of danger she and Tariq faced if they tried
to rescue the already trapped horses.

"Dear God!" Jesse moaned, her eyes frantically
searching the landscape for signs of some fire-fighters
or a county fire truck or two. But they were nowhere
in sight; there was only a wall of swiftly moving or-

ange flame that was diminishing its distance from the trapped horses in wide, hungry swaths.

A strong, maverick gust of wind blew away the clouds of smoke that were slowly encompassing Jesse and her mount. And for just a moment, she saw hope.

Below and behind the pond dam lay a narrow corridor of, as yet, unburned pasture. Jesse knew if she could reach it in time and turn the trapped and milling herd in the proper direction, their instinct for survival would take them through. With no further thought, Jesse rode her horse into the thick, burning cloud.

The horses neighed at her arrival. Their panic matched Jesse's own as she quickly circled the young horses, turning them to run blindly into the dense smoke. The wind blew madly down through the draw behind the pond and carried tiny bits of still-burning embers with it, feeding the already bottomless maw of blaze that kept threatening to swallow Jesse and the horses.

Suddenly, the young horses saw the break in the fire. They needed no further urging than Jesse's shout. They erupted as one into the narrowing path and ran in headlong flight, heads up, manes and tails flowing out behind them like the tails of kites caught in the whirlwind.

And then they were through the smoke, the threatening blaze now at their backs, taunting and teasing with imminent disaster as the strong winds kept blowing the fire across the prairie. There was nothing left for Jesse to do but outrun it. She bit back a sob of panic as a strong gust of wind pushed the fire almost beneath her horse's feet. She felt him jump and surge forward, felt the massive muscles bunch beneath her as she wrapped the reins around her wrists and leaned almost full-length across Tariq's powerful neck.

"Okay, boy," Jesse yelled in his ear. She kicked him sharply. "Take us home."

The great stallion leaped forward, his haunches bunched as his hooves dug into the dry, burning earth. And he ran as he'd never run before. He was running for his life, and taking Jesse with him.

King knew the fire had jumped the creek by the direction of the smoke. His stomach roiled and a pull in the depths of his gut told him what his mind refused to accept. He was going to be too late to help Jesse. Whatever happened was happening now, and he was helpless to stop it or aid her in any way. He was too far away. He hit the steering wheel in frustration with his fist, and pressed the gas pedal all the way to the floor.

The fire break was completed. Turner and Charlie had headed back to the ranch when Turner saw the gathering smoke billowing across the grass land west of the ranch.

"Charlie! It's jumped Salt Creek," Turner yelled over the tractor's noisy engine. "We've got to hurry!"

His words were no sooner said then he saw something else that made fingers of fear crawl down the neck of his shirt and grab at his heart. The big wooden gate in the pasture above the barn was wide open, fastened back against the fence to keep it from blowing shut. The only time they ever did that was when moving livestock. Turner knew what had happened without a second thought. Jesse had gone after the horses. He pushed the throttle forward on the big John Deere tractor, and headed for the ranch, bouncing the raised plow behind him in wild abandon. King would kill them all if anything happened to that girl.

Turner had no more than reached the machine shed when he saw the Jeep hurtling down the long driveway. He knew, somehow, that King was already aware of Jesse's danger.

The Jeep skidded sideways, sliding precariously through the loose dirt and gravel, before it finally came to a halt just in front of the corrals.

King vaulted from the Jeep, and Turner knew by the look on his face that he was almost out of his mind.

"She's gone, hasn't she?" King yelled, his voice cracking from smoke and stress.

"Boss, I didn't even know it until minutes ago when I saw the open gate. Did she go after the horses?" he asked.

"Hell, yes," King shouted, and turned around wildly, as if looking for an answer to his fears. "And I as good as told her to go. If anything happens to her, it'll be my fault."

His voice broke, and his dark eyes narrowed in frustration and fear as he watched the huge clouds of smoke the winds were pushing over the crest of the hill. There was no hesitation in his movements. He started toward the corral gate with every intention of taking the Jeep into the fire. But the volunteer fire-fighters' arrival momentarily stopped his progress.

"Looks like your firebreak might stop this, King," one of the men yelled as he jumped from the back of a pickup truck and waved a group of men into position, just in case the fire jumped the wide strip of plowed ground. Then he saw King McCandless running toward the gate leading into the fields. "Where are you going, man?" he yelled. "Don't be foolish. That firebreak will hold."

"Jesse," he yelled hoarsely, pointing toward the now visible flames behind the blowing smoke. "She's in there...somewhere. I'm going to get her."

Word spread through the crowd of men like the wild fire itself. A woman was trapped in there. They each watched in mounting horror at the wall of smoke that came rolling down the hill toward the barns. There was no way on earth that she'd live through that.

Suddenly, a sound came riding on the wind, stopping each and every man in his tracks. All eyes turned toward the hillside.

"Boss!" Turner called out, and pointed wildly in the direction of the fire. "Open the corral gates. She's bringin' em' in."

The wild thunder of horses' hooves and the occasional fear-laden whinny could be heard, along with the crackle and roar of the prairie fire. Then they burst through the smoke, running on the hands of the wind, toward the gleaming white walls of the barn and safety.

"There she comes! By God, there she comes!" he heard Turner shout, and King felt the bones in his legs turn to jelly. Fear for Jesse's safety expanded as he watched her tiny figure plastered to the back of his stallion.

The horses were crazed by the fire and the wild race against time. He knew it would take more than a miracle to stop the stampeding herd. He shook off his terror, his eyes fixed on Jesse and his horse. King pushed open the gates to the corral and then began to run.

Jesse didn't even know when they finally cleared the wall cloud of burning prairie and began the descent toward the ranch. Her arms and hands were nearly numb just from trying to stay mounted. So much smoke and ashes had blown into her eyes that they were pouring tears. She could only see through a watery veil, and heard the wild cheers of the men congregated at the edge of the plowed strip of ground before she saw them. When she did, her heart skipped a beat. She bit her lower lip to keep from screaming.

We made it! She could see the wall of white below, and the gate to the corral being pushed open to receive the thundering herd. Then, as quickly as her elation had soared, it now gave way to total terror. She'd made it out of the fire, but she knew she'd never be able to stop Tariq. A tiny moan slipped through her tightly clinched lips. She almost lost her seat as her concentration slipped.

King saw her falter, and terror such as he'd never known gave strength to his arms and legs.

The herd of horses had swerved toward the opening in the corral as surely as they'd run through the opening in the fire. But Tariq ran on, heading for the rails of the fence in wild abandon. He was going to jump...and when he did Jesse would be lost. King stood his ground and met the fear-crazed stallion head on.

King heard the pounding hooves coming nearer and nearer, heard the harsh, panting gasps of Tariq's tortured lungs, saw the horse's wild, red-rimmed eyes roll frantically at the man standing in his flight path. Just as the horse came thundering down upon him, just before he would go under the powerful hooves, King reached out, grabbed the side of Tariq's bridle, curled his fingers around the metal attached to the bit in the horse's mouth and hung on for Jesse...and for dear life.

Jesse only saw the top of his head, and then it looked as if he'd gone under Tariq's hooves. He disappeared from view. Jesse screamed, trying with all her waning strength to pull back on the reins wrapped tightly around her wrists.

The horse tried to rear, pawing wildly at the air with his front legs, but there was an unfamiliar weight tugging at his tender mouth and his struggle was unsuccessful. He fought and jumped, trying to dislodge the weight from his mouth and neck, but it was too much effort. Exhaustion finally took hold as he side-stepped across the plowed stretch of field and ran full tilt into the outstretched hands of the fire-fighters. He stood, head down, foam-flecked and singed, and began to shake, his tired muscles reacting violently to the sudden stop.

Jesse slumped over the saddle horn, and would have fallen onto the plowed ground had strong arms not reached out to catch her. She felt the tight strips of leather being gently unwound from her wrists. Her hands tingled and then began to ache as circulation began to flow.

The men were cheering and laughing, relieved at the happy ending to what had seemed certain disaster. Jesse's wild ride and bravery were nearly overshadowed by the life-threatening sacrifice King had made. They'd all witnessed him catch a stampeding stallion with his bare hands and pull him to a halt with sheer strength.

King couldn't think past the fact that he and Jesse were still alive. He held her cradled in his arms as if she were made of glass, and began to walk through the dry clods toward the barn. The fire would soon be out. The firebreak had stopped it. The horses were safe, milling about in a tight circle inside the corral as they calmed down.

Turner led the big white stallion past King, as he walked on, silently carrying his precious burden. Turner looked quickly away, ignoring the tears running down the big man's face, plowing little clean tracks through the dust and ashes coating his skin.

"Boss," he called back, without turning around to see if King was listening. "I'll tend to clean-up around here. You take her on to the house. See you tomorrow."

King heard, but could not acknowledge, the extent of his old foreman's thoughtfulness. He only knew he was never going to let Jesse out of his sight again.

Jesse felt his heartbeat, wild and erratic beneath her cheek, felt him shudder and then gather her closer. She sighed with relief and weariness, then closed her burning eyes. King was taking her home.

Chapter 11

The house was quiet—a cool, clean haven from the world outside that had nearly gone up in flames. Silence lengthened between King and Jesse until she could stand it no longer.

"King," she began, as he carried her through the living quarters toward the bedrooms. "I can walk, I think. Why don't…"

"No," he muttered, kicking open the door to his bedroom. "I may never put you down, Jesse Rose. I *know* I'm never letting you out of my sight again." His voice broke as he sank down on the bed and propped Jesse against his lap.

"King," she whispered, slowly sliding her arms around his neck. "I'm sorry. I didn't intend for this to happen." She leaned her face into the curve of his neck

and kissed a muscle twitching uncontrollably in his
jaw. "I thought you were...I thought you fell under..."

Tears of relief kept threatening to erupt, but she
couldn't cry. The tears were frozen in the horror of the
last few minutes when she'd imagined King dead.

"Hush," he whispered, and pulled her across his lap,
dangling her legs on either side until she was facing
him.

He cupped her face in his hands, leaned forward, and
pulled Jesse toward him. Not an inch of her face escaped the branding touch of his lips as he lay claim to
the woman he'd so nearly lost.

Jesse's heart soared. She wanted to laugh. She
wanted to cry. Instead, she pulled him closer and captured his next kiss with desperation. Every taste, every
pull of his lips against her skin sent pinpoints of heat
shooting to the center of her being. She felt King thread
his fingers through her hair as he, once more, captured
her lips. It wasn't enough and he clasped her roughly
under her arms and pulled her closer, moaning in response to her mouth that was opening slowly beneath
his touch.

King's breathing was coming in harsh, hurtful gulps
as he struggled with the need to breathe and have Jesse
all at the same time. Finally, he reluctantly pulled
away, and gently ran his thumb across her lips.

"My God, Jesse Rose. I nearly lost you today. I
nearly lost you," he whispered huskily, running his
hands gently over and over her body, not believing that

she was still in one piece. "Nothing would have mattered to me if I'd lost you, baby. Don't you understand that?" He leaned his head forward until their foreheads were gently touching, and gripped her firmly around the waist, "I love you, Jesse. I love you so much it makes my teeth ache. I watch you laugh, and forget what I was going to say. I watch you walk, and forget what I was going to do. I watch you sleep, and know that nothing in my life is worth keeping unless you're beside me."

Then his voice broke, and Jesse felt him shudder and begin to tremble beneath her.

"I need to love you, baby. I've held back too long now. I want you, Jess." His eyes darkened with emotion and he bent down and buried his face in the valley between her breasts. "If you don't want this, you're going to have to stop me, because I don't think I can stop myself."

Jesse slid from his lap and began to walk away.

King numbly watched his world coming to an end. He couldn't think as he watched her leave him.

Dear God, no! he thought. It felt like he'd been kicked in the stomach.

Jesse reached out and turned the lock on his bedroom door. She pivoted around to face him with tears in her eyes, a smile on her lips, and began to unbutton her dust-coated shirt and jeans.

"Bath...or shower?" she whispered, as she walked out of the pile of blue denim at her feet and let her shirt drop beside it.

She was in his arms and off her feet, as King whirled her around the room.

Steam swirled inside the walls of the shower, coating the sliding glass doors until Jesse's vision was nearly obliterated. The water ran in a warm torrent down her body, washing away the remnants of her wild ride through the burning prairie. She reached up to the shelf above her head for the bottle of shampoo. Her hands came away empty. King's deep, husky voice behind her stopped her search.

"Let me, honey," he coaxed, and pulled her away from the water's swift flow.

She smelled the sharp, fresh scent of the lemon shampoo permeate the enclosure, and felt his hands begin to knead through the smoky tangles of her hair, working the shampoo into a rich, cleansing lather. She sighed, and leaned back against his chest, letting those talented hands work their magic on her tired, aching body. Her eyes closed in reflex as his hands continued down the back of her neck, then around, cradling her breasts in each hand as he captured stray bits of lather.

"Feel good?" he whispered against her ear, and was rewarded with a tiny moan of pleasure that fired an answering echo within himself.

He didn't know how *Jesse* felt, but she felt *fine* to him. He stepped forward, placing them both under the pounding force of the spray. Lather ran between their bodies, swirling around their feet, before it disappeared down the drain. King quickly repeated the process on himself, closing his eyes against the treacherous soap, and nearly lost his footing when Jesse's hands began an intimate foray that sent good sense down the drain with the shampoo.

"Wait a minute, sweetheart," he begged, grabbing at a towel as he turned off the water. "You don't know what you're doing." He smiled seductively at the blue-eyed nymph with the curious hands.

Jesse leaned back against the door of the shower and let her eyes continue what her hands began.

"Oh," she drawled, as she watched his body tense and harden with desire, "I think I do."

King's sharply indrawn breath and the fire that kindled in his eyes were Jesse's only warnings. He had her out of the shower and dry before another thought had time to form.

"So," he whispered, as he laid her down in the middle of his bed, then stood back and feasted his eyes on the tantalizing thought of crawling in beside her, "you think you know what you're doing?"

"No," she answered quietly, and her honesty shook his resolve. "But I know what I want *you* to do, King."

Breath constricted in his throat as he knelt beside her and ran his fingers around the instep of her foot, then let them travel the inside of her leg, up...up...until he paused at her threshold, his dark eyes promising passion.

Jesse shuddered, and shifted uneasily on the bed, mesmerized by the touch of his hands and the knowledge that this magnificent man with the magic touch was finally going to make love to her.

"I know what you want, baby," he groaned, stretching full length beside her. "That's what I want, too. I promised, remember?"

His mouth captured a rosy nub, and his hand another, as he began a journey across Jesse that would culminate in a promise kept.

His hands, his mouth, and the weight of his body on hers drove sanity and reason away. Jesse wanted to touch him. She needed to watch him watching her. But she knew if she opened her eyes, or turned loose of the bed beneath her, or moved an inch away from the seeking, pulsing pressure of his body, she'd fly away so far she'd never come down.

Every promise he whispered in her ear would then come true as he stroked and touched, nipped and tasted. Spasm after spasm of building heat waves made an ache so fierce that Jesse begged for release she didn't know how to achieve.

"King, please," she moaned, "tell me what to do."

She moved beneath him, seeking, pushing, yearning for something. Then she felt her lower body lift off the bed as King's hand dipped past a boundary no man had ever passed.

She gasped, let loose her grip on the bed, and dug her fingers into the still-damp tangles of his hair.

King's breath was coming in quick, painful draughts, as he struggled to hold back an overwhelming need to disappear inside the woman beneath him. The softness below would soothe his own aching body, but still he waited as he teased at the throb beneath his fingers.

"Tell you what to do?" he asked, and took the question from her lips with one swoop of his mouth. "You don't need to do anything. I'll tell you what *I'm* going to do, baby," he whispered against her lips. "I'm going to make you forget every man you've ever known, every man who's even crossed your path and wished. I don't want anyone in your life now but me."

He lifted himself over her, nearly blind with a need to dissolve into this woman below him.

Her soft whisper barely penetrated through the blood thundering in his ears, but when it did, it stopped him cold.

"I don't have to forget what never was," Jesse said, and slid her hands down the tightly bunched muscles tensing along his back. Her hands slid around his waist, urging him to finish what they'd started.

King blinked, shook his head slowly, then leaned forward, collapsing his entire weight as he buried his face in the curve of her neck.

"What in hell are you telling me, Jesse Rose?" he pleaded, then lifted himself away, focusing on the clear blue gaze beneath him. He was falling into space, weightless and out of control.

"That I love you, King McCandless. And that I've waited a lifetime to show you how much."

"No...no, Jess," King groaned in disbelief, suddenly afraid to move, yet knowing he had to. It was just that this gift was so much more than he'd expected...so much more than he deserved.

"Please," Jesse begged, and felt his silent answer as he slowly surged forward.

It was only a tiny, fleeting pressure that erupted into one blinding flash of pain, and then the sensation of emptiness Jesse had felt for so long completely disappeared as King swelled within her.

King winced, regretting the need for the tiny gasp he heard, and saw her eyes flutter as she bit against her lower lip to keep from crying aloud.

"I'm sorry. So sorry, baby," he muttered, and bent down, placing kisses of repentance on her eyelids and down the sides of her mouth. "But I can promise you this, it's the last pain I'll ever willingly give you. From now on, Jesse, it's nothing but pleasure."

His body tensed as he took a deep, agonized breath, then began to move slowly in a rhythm as old as time. Just before words became more than he could form, he managed to whisper his promise into the silence of the room before Jesse took him into paradise. "Sweet, sweet, pleasure."

Duncan watched the smoke from his window high above Tulsa, and judged the location to be near, if not actually on, the Double M. He knew it was a grass fire—a big one, judging by the size of the smoke clouds. His eyes narrowed, his lips thinned, and the planes of his face angled and flattened until he was barely recognizable.

"The whole damn place can go up in smoke for all I care," he muttered.

He walked to the bar and poured himself another drink. It seemed these days that that was all he was able to do—drink to avoid what he knew lay in wait. He walked back to the window with his drink in hand and stood silently, debating with himself about the wisdom of going out to the ranch to help. Finally, what was left of his conscience rallied. He spun about, intent on driving to the ranch, when the phone rang and stopped him squarely in the middle of the living room floor.

Now he had to decide whether to answer it or let it ring. It could be a number of people, all of whom he owed money, and he nearly didn't answer. But the persistent, shrill tone won out over his jangled nerves.

"McCandless," he said shortly, then let his drink spill slowly from his glass onto the carpeted floor.

"I know who it is, Boss," the voice whined. "And you know who this is, too. Damn it, you promised to come back. I got hungry, man. I needed to eat, and I needed medicine."

"What the hell do you want?" Duncan asked, his voice low and angry. "And where are you?"

"You know what I want. I need cash. I'm here…in town. And I ain't got no way to disappear. They're lookin' for me all over. You got to help me. After all, this was your idea," he said accusingly.

"It wasn't my idea to hurt her," he said all too softly. "And it wasn't my damned idea to go passing hot checks and get caught on video at the same time, you stupid son-of-a-bitch. I don't *have* any money, thanks to you. And you better get the hell out of Tulsa, because I'll finish what Jesse started if you don't. Do I make myself, clear?''

Lynch shuddered at the still, ominous quality in the man's voice, and knew the moment of truth had arrived. Now not only were the cops after him for attempted murder and kidnapping, but this man, a formidable foe, also had good reason to want him dead. With one last act of bravado, he whined, "Well, if the cops get me, you'll be next."

"No, I won't," Duncan sneered. "I'm not stupid. There's absolutely nothing linking me to you, or the crime, except your word. Who do you think the cops will believe—a concerned member of the family or a murdering crook?''

"You bastard!" Lynch cried. "You got to help me."

"Where are you?" Duncan asked quietly.

Suddenly, Wiley Lynch knew he'd said too much. He had pushed a man he was mortally afraid of too far.

"Never mind," Lynch muttered. "I'll get myself out of town. I'll hitch a ride…something. Just forget I asked, okay, Boss?''

Just then another truckload of livestock pulled into the stockyards by the pay phone Wiley Lynch was using. The constant bellow and lowing of the load of cattle and the truck's shifting gears echoed into the receiver.

"Okay, Boss?" he repeated. But the line went dead

as Duncan McCandless gently placed the phone back on the hook.

Lynch stood, staring in horror at the milling crowd of people around him and began to shake. McCandless knew where he was! He dropped the receiver, letting it dangle in the wind and heat, and began to run in a scurrying fashion back to the pile of shipping crates behind the sale barn, unaware of several people's curious, suspicious stares. First chance he got, he would be on a cattle truck heading west.

King lay quietly, absorbing the rise and fall of Jesse's breasts beneath his hand, and watched the first ray of morning lighten the shadows in his room. He raised up on one elbow and propped his head in his hands so he could watch her sleep.

Her lashes lay like thick, curly fans on her windburned cheeks, and King felt a fierce wave of protectfulness sweep over him at the thought of anyone, or anything, ever hurting Jesse again.

She was so small and fragile in appearance, yet King knew what a strong, fierce spirit she possessed. She was more than a match for his physical strength. She'd proven that over and over throughout the night as King would take her to the brink of passion, pushing her right to the edge of reason, and then, just before she felt herself fly into a million pieces beneath his mouth and hands, he'd gather her into his arms, and with one wild thrust send them both falling through mindless space.

He leaned over, gently ran the tip of his finger along the line of her slightly swollen lower lip, humble with the knowledge of what Jesse had saved, then given to him last night. *Please God, may I never make her sorry.*

He inhaled sharply at the quick, intense reaction of his body as Jesse rolled over and buried her face against his chest. He was instantly hard, throbbing with a need he knew only Jesse could fill. Her arms slid around him as she pulled herself against the thrust of his body, and King felt himself lose it as she opened her mouth, nuzzled against his chest, took a hard brown nipple between her teeth and pressed lightly.

"Does that feel as good to you as it does to me?" Jesse whispered.

King's sudden intake of breath told her what he could not. She did it once more for good measure, and found herself on top of his hard, aching body. Jesse had one swift look at the wild flare of passion in his eyes before he groaned and slid into her.

"Does *that* feel as good to you as it does to me?" he asked in return, and pulled her hips down tightly across him.

Jesse gasped and moaned, as he began moving beneath her in a soft, tantalizing thrust.

"Yes, yes, yes," she mumbled. And then she forgot why she'd answered as King took her on a ride she'd never forget.

It was some time later before either of them could move, and even later before they could think. Finally the phone rang, ending their lethargy. King reluctantly released Jesse and rolled over to answer.

It was Maggie and she was on her way home. That message had them both on their feet and hurrying to dress. Maggie would know soon enough about the new turn of events between them, but they wanted to tell her not show her. By the time Maggie arrived, they had coffee brewed and breakfast waiting on the table.

"My stars," she announced as she came through the front door. "Are you two all right? It looks like the place nearly went up in flames yesterday."

She was referring to the huge, blackened swath covering the hillside. Before either King or Jesse could answer, Maggie took another, closer look at the expressions on their faces. She smiled slyly. "Or maybe it wasn't the Double M that went up in flames last night. Is there something you two want to tell me?"

Guilt painted an embarrassed blush on King's face. He stuttered. Then he started to explain, grinned sheepishly and pulled her into his arms, whirling her around the living room floor, much to her surprise and glee.

"You're not the only love of my life, woman. Put your bag down and come to breakfast. We'll fill you in on what you think you've missed." Then he added, "At least part of it."

The last dish was washed and put away as King came back through the door. He'd been outside, overseeing the damage they'd sustained, and issuing orders for the day.

"Jesse Rose," he called, slamming the door shut

behind him. "If you're barefoot, grab your shoes. We're going to Tulsa to pick up the cattle check at the stockyard."

"But I was going to help..." she started to say, when he pulled her off her feet and into his arms, fixing her with an unwavering stare.

"If you think I'm leaving you here alone again, you're crazy, woman. You can't be trusted, and I'm too tired to rescue you again today. Okay?"

Jesse smiled, placed a kiss in the vicinity of his left ear, and whispered softly so that the grinning Maggie couldn't overhear, "How come you're so tired?" she teased. "Was it something I said...or was it something I did?"

"Witch," he growled, and set her down before he embarrassed them both. "Get your damn shoes."

King pulled the Lincoln carefully between stock trailers and semi-trucks that were loading and unloading droves of milling, bawling, cattle. He parked between a Cadillac and a rusted-out pickup truck.

There was less class-consciousness among farmers and ranchers than any other group of working men in America. Whether they ran a big spread or a nickel-and-dime operation on weekends only, they all faced the same frustrations and joys, and at one time or another they all wound up with manure on their boots. Ranching had a way of equalizing men.

"My check will be at the office, Jess," he said, as he parked. "Come with me."

"I know," Jesse chided, as she scooted across the seat. "You don't trust me."

"I love you, baby," he whispered, and dipped his head to steal a kiss from her pouting lips. "Trust *me,* okay?"

The hot breeze whipped the skirt of Jesse's light green sundress around her legs and outlined her slim body in a tantalizing caress. King jammed his hat down on his head and guided Jesse between the parked and moving vehicles.

"Whew," he muttered, as they stepped quickly inside, shutting the wind and heat and the ever-present smell of manure and diesel smoke outside. "You can sit here, Jesse," he said, indicating a row of assorted wood and metal folding chairs outside the cashier's window. "It may take a while. They may not have the check ready. I don't mind telling you, it's just luck that I hauled that herd off to market when I did. The fire would have taken some of them for sure."

Then, realizing what he'd said about the fire, he frowned. Ignoring any curious stares or whispers from anyone present, he cupped her face in his hands and tilted it toward him.

"I wasn't lucky yesterday, Jesse. I was blessed. But not because the stock was saved." His voice was low and husky; his dark eyes filled with promise and regret.

"I know, King," Jesse said, and caressed the hand cupping her cheek. "It's okay. Go on and get in line. I'll just wait here." She took a seat between two grinning women who'd witnessed their interchange.

* * *

Lynch couldn't believe his eyes. It was the boss, kissing the same woman he'd hired him to snatch.

"What the hell is goin' on here?" he whined to himself, and slipped behind the pair as they hurried toward the offices.

He'd been trying ever since daybreak to sneak aboard an empty cattle truck, but so far had remained unsuccessful. The drivers were careful to search their empty trailers before taking off. They had no desire to haul hitchhikers. It was dangerous, and it was illegal.

Now Lynch wondered if it wasn't fate that made him miss a ride. Maybe he could still get some money. McCandless wouldn't want to cause a scene in front of the woman. He rubbed his hands together gleefully, and stayed just out of sight as King and Jesse entered the offices. Now all he had to do was wait.

"Hey, boy!" a loud, boisterous voice boomed out behind King and Jesse as they left the sale barn on their way back to the car. "How 'bout a loan?"

King grinned and turned to see one of his dad's old friends.

"*You* need a loan?" King teased. "Not in this lifetime, Booster. You could loan money to the federal government and never miss it."

The grizzled old cowboy's cackle was nearly drowned out by the noise of a truck pulling away from the stockyards.

"Here, honey," King said, as he handed Jesse the

car keys. "Go on and get in out of the heat. I'll just say 'hi' to Booster."

"Okay," Jesse said. "Give him my love."

"I'll tell him you said 'hi', too," King growled. "Your love's all mine."

Jesse felt her face flame along with an answering fire in the pit of her stomach. *Lord have mercy,* she thought, as she headed for the car's cool comfort, *I've created a monster.* And then she grinned to herself. *And he's all mine.*

King was momentarily trapped between two long, semi-trailer trucks, one coming, one going. He stepped back against the bumper of a parked truck and ducked his head as the dust boiled up his nostrils and into his eyes. When a man behind him began to speak it startled him. He didn't even know anyone was around. He turned sideways, blinking rapidly as he tried to see past the film of dust coating his vision.

"Hey, Boss," the man whined. "What's the damn deal? I saw you kiss her. If you was on them kinda terms, how come you wanted her snatched?"

King couldn't believe what he was hearing, nor could he believe who he thought he was seeing.

"What in hell?" he muttered as he rubbed his eyes, anxiously trying to remove the dirt and grit. The man was still there...and he looked just like...

"I need some dough," the man said, and hitched at his pants as they slid down his skinny hips. "Don't tell me again that you're broke. I just saw you go in the office and pick up that big fat check. All I need is a little to get me out of town. I swear you'll never hear from me again. I won't tell no one about our deal. I swear it. I know I screwed up, but you should have told me that LeBeau woman was no sissy.''

It was when he mentioned Jesse's name that King was certain who was talking to him. But he couldn't get past the horror building inside his mind. Why did Lynch think he knew him?

''Lynch? Wiley Lynch?'' King growled huskily, and started toward him.

''What the...?'' Lynch muttered, and felt with certainty that he'd just made a terrible, terrible mistake. He didn't know that deep, unfamiliar voice. He knew the face, but not the voice.

''Who are you?'' he asked, and began to stumble backward. ''You're not McCandless!''

''Yes, I am, you son-of-a-bitch,'' King growled. ''I'm the one who was going to cough up the half million. And I know who you are too. You're dead.''

Wiley Lynch took one last, wild look at the big man, and began to run. He didn't have to look behind to see if McCandless was following him. He could hear him. He knew it would take a miracle to escape the wrath of the big man who was quickly closing the distance between them.

''Miss LeBeau?'' a man asked, as he stepped from behind King's Lincoln and flashed his badge.

The sunlight caught and held on the shiny metal as Jesse looked up, startled. Suddenly she was afraid. The man, so out of place in suit and tie, took her firmly by the elbow.

"Oklahoma State Bureau of Investigation," he said, as they walked quickly toward another group of men all dressed in similar fashion. A familiar, short, stocky figure emerged from the men and took Jesse by the hand.

"Miss LeBeau," he greeted her. "It's been a while. You look much better than the last time I saw you. Would you please come with me? The men here have a job to finish, and you and McCandless out of the line of fire, so to speak."

"Captain Shockey?" Jesse said, stunned to see the Missouri policeman here in Oklahoma.

The implications of his presence began to dawn on her, and she spun around, frantically searching the crowded parking lot for King.

"We got a tip last night that Lynch might be here," he said. "Couldn't believe my eyes when I saw you two come out of the offices. Fate plays funny tricks sometimes."

"King," she asked, and clutched his arm in fear. "He was right behind me, and now I don't see him."

Her voice began to shake, and her legs went weak.

One of the OSBI men frowned at her statement. He motioned for some of the men to follow, then one of the trucks blocking their vision finally moved. He stood transfixed for mere seconds before he began to run.

"It's Lynch," he yelled, as they started in fast pursuit, "and McCandless is after him."

The men split up, running in parallel paths, hoping to converge on the fleeing suspect should he try to escape down one of the many narrow paths between the dozens of holding corrals where the livestock were kept until sold at auction.

Jesse started to follow, but was pulled back by Shockey's strong, unyielding grasp.

"Let the men do their job, Miss LeBeau," he urged. "You stay here with me. I'm here by invitation only. This is out of my jurisdiction. But I like to see the end of a case for myself."

She couldn't think past the horrible fear that poured into her brain. All she could remember was that man, and his knife, and the pain. Now King was in danger. She leaned limply against the hot fender of the unmarked police car and began to shake.

Twice King almost had a hand on him, and then Lynch would pivot and dart down another path between the holding pens. A black rage kept him going, unswerving in his determination that this man would not escape again. Not this time. He could feel Lynch's fear. He heard the choking gasps for breath, and knew Lynch was tiring. But he still managed to stay just out of King's reach. Lynch was running for his life.

The wind and heat, the stench of manure, the cattle's uneasy lowing as the race among them heightened brought a growing certainty to Wiley Lynch that he'd reached a point of no return. He wasn't going to escape this big, angry man. His lungs burned. His legs ached. Then he saw it! A slim chance, *but* a chance. He gathered all of his remaining strength, and made one long leap toward a big semi pulling an empty cattle trailer out of the loading chute. If he could just get a handhold on the slat-sided truck, maybe, just maybe…

King realized Lynch's intention and dived for his feet just as he jumped. He felt the dust on Lynch's shoes come away in his hands, but he missed and fell face down in the dust, inches away from his goal. He looked up in dismay, certain that he was going to see Lynch's escape. Instead, he watched in horror as Lynch misjudged his vault and fell under the rolling eighteen-wheeler.

Suddenly hands were all over King, pulling him to his feet. Dozens of people kept asking him if he was all right.

"What the hell?" he muttered. He was tired, winded and sick at heart at the growing suspicion inside him.

"OSBI, Mr. McCandless," one of them answered. "We have Miss LeBeau. She's fine."

"Well, you can't say the same for that bastard," King said, and pointed to what was left of Wiley Lynch.

He pushed roughly past the gathering group of by-standers, who looked on in horror at what they judged to be a terrible accident. King headed back to his car with a wild, fierce glint in his eyes. This wasn't over yet.

Chapter 12

As word spread of the accident, gathering crowds obscured Jesse's view. She struggled within Shockey's grasp, unwilling to wait quietly while her world might be coming to an end. She could hear the rising volume of voices as more people became aware of the events that had just taken place. Many were not aware that a chase had been in progress, or that the police were already on the scene. Most of the police were in plain clothes and driving unmarked vehicles.

"Please," Jesse pleaded. "I just need to go find him." But she could tell by the determined look on Shockey's face that her plea was useless.

Suddenly King emerged from the pushing crowd of onlookers, and Jesse caught back a sob of relief. She pulled away from Shockey's restraint and began to run.

Yet the closer she came to King, the more a different kind of panic set in. King didn't even see her, wasn't aware that she was anywhere close, until Jesse grabbed him by the arm as he started to pass by her.

"King!" she cried. "What happened? Did they catch Lynch? Are you all right?"

King looked blindly down at her hand, then up at the worried expression on her face. A black hole was opening in his mind. He knew he should answer, but he couldn't focus on anything but the growing certainty that he knew who Lynch's "Boss" was.

He shrugged away from Jesse's grasp, and continued toward his car in single-minded determination. Then he remembered, and turned back to Jesse, as she stood watching his actions in stunned silence.

"Give me the keys," he whispered, and swallowed an urge to let his rage take hold.

Jesse began to shake. She clutched the keys tightly in her hands and refused to acknowledge King's command. He wasn't going to shut her out like this. She wouldn't allow it.

"What's wrong with you, King? What happened? Please, sweetheart," she pleaded, as an overwhelming fear began to replace her reason. Something was still very wrong.

"Jesse," he shouted, "give me the damn keys."

Shockey walked up just in time to hear their heated exchange, and knew trouble wasn't over after all. This man was out of control.

"Not until you tell me what happened," Jesse

screamed back at him. "This concerns me as much as it does you." Huge tears gathered and began spilling down her cheeks as she clutched the car keys tighter against her breast.

King wouldn't allow himself to think about Jesse. He had a growing horror within him that replaced everything but a need to hear for himself that what he feared was wrong. It had to be.

"Lynch is dead," he finally muttered. Then his voice rose in angry volume as he shouted, "But he recognized me." King spun around wildly, his boots kicking up dust as he pounded his fist on the hood of his car. "He thought he knew me!"

"I don't understand," Jesse whispered, clutching the keys as an anchor against the suspicion that suddenly started the world spinning around her. "He doesn't know you...does he?"

"No...he doesn't know *me*." King muttered, his throat tight and aching as he continued. "But, Jesse...he knows someone who looks like me." He watched comprehension hit Jesse in the face with a resounding slap. "And," he continued, "he called him 'Boss.'"

Jesse staggered, struck dumb by the implication of King's accusation. She let the keys fall from her hands as her knees gave way.

Shockey reached out and caught her as King snagged the car keys just before they hit the dirt.

"Take care of her," King ordered, and started to stalk away.

"You wait a minute," Captain Shockey ordered. "I want to know what's going on here." But his words were useless as King backed the car away from the stunned pair and drove off in a cloud of dust.

"Oh, God!" Jesse moaned, and buried her face in her hands. She had to do something. She couldn't let King get to Duncan. If he did, one of them would die. Either King would kill Duncan, or he'd die trying. Anyway she looked at it, she was going to lose King.

"Miss LeBeau," Shockey ordered, grabbing her shoulders and shaking her gently. "Get hold of yourself and tell me what in hell all that was about."

"Duncan," she mumbled, and started pulling Shockey toward the cars. "We've got to hurry," she began to sob. "King has gone to find Duncan, and if he does, he'll kill him."

"Who the hell is Duncan, and why would King want to kill him?" he asked, allowing Jesse to pull him along as they talked. It was obvious something more was involved. Maybe he was about to find the accomplice.

"Duncan is King's uncle," Jesse muttered. "Please, we've got to hurry!"

"Why would King want to kill his uncle, and what did he mean by Lynch recognizing him?"

"Lynch recognized King, at least he thought he did," Jesse answered, "because King and Duncan could pass for identical twins."

Shockey's hesitance was driving her mad. She screamed aloud as Shockey stopped stubbornly in front of her. "Lynch called King 'Boss.' Don't you see? He got them mixed up. Please, we have to hurry."

The implication was sinking into Shockey's analytical mind as he yanked Jesse into the car seat beside him.

"Yes, girl, I'm beginning to," he answered. "Now give me an address fast. We're going to need help to stop that man."

He wrote down the address Jesse gave him, and grabbed his radio mike. The Tulsa police were going to have to help. He'd never make it in time to stop King McCandless.

King never knew how he got to Duncan's apartment. He didn't even bother to park properly. He just stopped, left the keys in the ignition, and got out of the car in a trance-like state. He could hear sirens in the distance, warning all who got in the way of their impending progress, but King was past rational thinking. He had to see Duncan face to face; he had to hear him admit what he feared was true, or deny it. King couldn't think past that. He couldn't let himself think about retribution.

His gut twisted in a knot of despair as he punched the twelfth-floor button in the elevator and swallowed the choking rage that rose bitterly in his throat. When the door opened at the twelfth floor, he had to tell himself to move. King knew now that each step he took would be bringing him close to the end of the world as he knew it.

He heard the elevator door open down the hall as he arrived at Duncan's apartment, but he ignored it. All his being was focused on the door in front of him. He took a deep breath, doubled up his fist, and hammered loudly.

"Duncan!" he shouted. "Open the door!" No one responded.

This time, when he pounded loudly on the door, he issued an ultimatum.

"Duncan! Open the damn door, or I'll kick it in."

There was an ominous silence before Duncan spoke sarcastically. "It's not locked, nephew. Do the civilized thing, and use the doorknob, please."

King twisted the knob and slammed the door back against the wall as he entered. His heart jerked to a full stop at the sight before him. He realized then that his worst fears were probably true.

Duncan was half standing, half sitting on a bar stool with a nearly empty bottle of bourbon in one hand, and a pistol in the other. He cocked an eyebrow at the big, angry man before him, the two policeman who followed him through the door, and waved the pistol in their general direction.

"Come in, come in," he called loudly. "I wasn't expecting you." Then he muttered to himself. "Or maybe I was. At any rate, you're here. What can I do for you?"

King looked around in surprise at the men behind him, and then back at Duncan, ignoring the officers' advice to take cover.

The police looked at each other, uncertain how to defuse the situation without someone getting hurt. One of them called out forcefully to Duncan McCandless. "Drop your gun, mister! Whatever's going on here can be settled without violence. Let me have your gun, then we'll talk about this."

Duncan smiled, ignoring their presence, and turned his attention to his nephew.

King spoke in short, clipped sentences, his husky voice so strained it wasn't much more than a whisper.

"Lynch is dead," King said, watching Duncan's face for something…anything…that would tell him he was wrong.

"Well, now," Duncan drawled. "That's good news, isn't it? That calls for a drink." He tipped his head back, tilted the bourbon bottle, and let the fiery liquid run slowly down his throat.

King never blinked. He never moved. But his hands clinched and unclinched at his side as he watched Duncan deteriorate before his eyes. It was a strange sensation. Almost like watching himself die.

"He called me 'Boss,'" King said softly. "Now why would he do that, Duncan? Why did he think he knew me?"

Duncan sat staring at the men before him. When the policemen started forward, he quietly aimed his pistol at King's chest and muttered, "Because he's a fool."

The police stopped instantly as the armed man took aim at King. But their guns remained pointed at the man by the bar. There was just no way they could disarm him without endangering the unarmed civilian, so they stood by, waiting anxiously for the armed man to make a mistake, or have a change of heart and put down his weapon.

"Why?" King asked, fury and betrayal in his posture and voice.

"Why?" Duncan repeated, and then his entire surface charm vanished. His face and posture changed. Suddenly he didn't look like King at all. He looked old and beaten.

"Because! Because you were born with what I wanted. What I deserved," he snarled. "Andrew was *my* brother before he was *your* father. You were born with *my* face...and they named *you* the 'King.' It wasn't fair. It wasn't fair."

King was stunned. He had to force himself not to shout as he spoke. "You blamed me for being born?" he growled in disbelief. "You spent...no...wasted your life hating me for an accident of birth? You pitiful son-of-a-bitch. I knew you were weak. I just didn't know you were stupid."

His taunt struck home as Duncan stood and glared furiously at the man he should have been. "Shut up," he warned, and took steadier aim at the third button on King's shirt.

"Back off, mister," the police said to King, but he ignored them as well as their order.

"Go ahead," King shouted, losing what was left of his control. "Shoot an unarmed man. I know you're capable. Anyone who'd use an innocent woman just to get back at me would do anything."

Duncan's face crumpled. For the first time, King saw genuine regret.

"She wasn't supposed to get hurt," he muttered. "He wasn't supposed to touch her."

"No?" King drawled sarcastically. "You were just going to kidnap her, scare her to death, cause her mental anguish for the rest of her life, but you weren't going to hurt her? What the hell kind of a twisted plot is that?"

"Well," Duncan sneered, "it wasn't smart. I'll admit that. But after all, what did you expect? I'm not the 'King.' So," he continued, "where does that leave us? I have no intention of going to jail and watching you walk away with everything, including Jesse."

King started forward, taking each step with controlled deliberation.

"Now's your chance," he snarled back in Duncan's face. "Pull the damn trigger, and get your misery over with."

"No!" a policeman shouted at King.

"Drop your weapon," the other ordered Duncan.

But the big man didn't stop advancing, and his mirror image remained, gun aimed, poised at the edge of making the last big mistake of his life.

Duncan blinked, startled that King was no longer under his control. He felt a sick, sinking feeling start at the bottom of his boots and crawl steadily upwards toward the huge knot of horror stuck in his throat. Now he had to make a choice, and he knew he had none left.

Duncan took unsteady aim, cocked the pistol, and called aloud in a jeering fashion, "The King is dead, long live the King."

A shot rang out. King stopped, his next step forgotten as the wide, spreading pain tightened around his chest. A denial of rage erupted from his mouth, but it was too late. He watched, horrified, as Duncan dropped limply to the floor, the life in his eyes disappearing as a pool of blood appeared beneath him.

Duncan McCandless, as usual, had taken the easy way out of a bad situation. He'd taken his own life.

"Aw, hell," one of the policemen muttered as they pushed past King's frozen figure. "Get an ambulance," he ordered, and his partner quickly responded.

Neither man had time to spend assuring King there was nothing that could have prevented this. When a crazy man has a loaded gun, someone's bound to get hurt. He could have just as easily turned it on them.

King turned and walked blindly toward the open door into the hall as the pain in his chest expanded into his mind. He felt helpless, uncertain, and betrayed in a way he'd never imagined.

The arrival of paramedics and OSBI officers clogged the narrow hallway as King wandered aimlessly toward the elevator. He had to get away from this nightmare. The only thing that was keeping him from coming apart was the thought of Jesse. She was out there... somewhere. And he knew he had to find her.

* * *

"What's happening?" Jesse asked nervously, as Captain Shockey maneuvered his way through Tulsa traffic, a red light on the dash of his car flashing a warning to allow him easier access. Jesse could hear the traffic on the police radio, but nearly everything was in code. She couldn't decipher their messages, yet the look on Shockey's face told Jesse something was wrong. She was afraid of his answer.

"Police and paramedics are on the scene," he replied gruffly.

"Paramedics?" Jesse felt sick to her stomach. It was almost more than she could ask. "Someone is hurt?"

Shockey hitched his position in the car seat, trying to find a cooler, more comfortable spot. But the sun coming through the windows beat out the faltering air conditioner's weak airflow, and the seats in these cars weren't ever going to be comfortable. One way or another, a policeman was always on a hot seat. Finally, he cleared his throat and blurted out, "Someone's not hurt," he replied. "Someone is dead."

"Not King," she moaned, and buried her face in her hands. It wasn't King. She couldn't face it if it was. "Hurry, please!" She choked back a sob, and gripped the armrest on the car door until her fingers turned white.

There were so many official vehicles in the apartment parking lot that Shockey had trouble turning into the entryway. Jesse looked frantically from man to man in the milling crowd around the cars and in the doorway. She saw nothing but uniforms.

Shockey hit the brakes, flashing his badge as an officer momentarily halted their progress. Jesse took the opportunity to bolt from the car. She was out and pushing her way through the policeman before Shockey had unbuckled his seat belt. Her heart was pounding so viciously against her ribcage that it hurt to breathe. Fear weakened her legs so that each step she took was a test of endurance. Yet she continued blindly toward the darkened doorway, shaded by a wide, striped awning over the walkway. More than one officer noted the pretty, dark-haired woman in the green dress darting through the crowd, but each time a hand stretched out to restrain her, she would elude the order to stop.

King saw a flash of green coming through the crowd, and felt all the anxiety of the last few minutes pour from him in a rush. It was Jesse. He fixed on that sundress with desperation, and came out of the shadowed doorway into the sun.

Jesse saw him pause, saw the stunned, blank expression and the almost aimless stride. Then she saw him focus and start toward her with unwavering determination. She was in his arms!

King clutched desperately, tangling his fingers in her hair as he drew strength and sanity just from holding her against his heart. He couldn't talk. It was beyond him to tell her, at least…not yet. He couldn't admit to himself the festering guilt that was beginning to spread inside him. How had he been so blind? How could he have been so unaware of such vicious, demented hate? Maybe if he'd noticed sooner? There had to have been signals over the years. Maybe…just maybe he could have prevented this. But it was too late to speculate. Jesse had nearly died…and Duncan *was* dead. And in some way, King had decided, it was all his fault.

Jesse felt him begin to shake, felt the desperation in his grasp, and tightening her hold on him, breathing a prayer of thanksgiving that he was alive and in her arms.

Minutes passed. They were surrounded by OSBI and Captain Shockey, all wanting answers to their questions. They wanted to know what had tipped him off. How had he realized who was the mastermind behind Jesse's failed kidnapping? Finally King had enough.

"We're going home," he said tersely, daring anyone to argue. "If you have any other questions, come to the ranch, or call. You have our number."

No one disagreed as King ushered Jesse toward the car.

"King," Jesse said. "Let me drive."

He looked down at the concern on her face, and the way she kept holding back tears. His mind was blanking out. Whenever there was a lull in the conversation, King saw that last look on Duncan's face over and over. He knew if he got behind the wheel of the car, he wouldn't see traffic. He wouldn't hear anything but Duncan's last accusations flung into his face.

He nodded, opened the door on the driver's side for Jesse, then hurried around to get in. A KTUL camera crew had just arrived. He had no desire to be on the six o'clock news.

"We're home," Jesse said quietly. She pulled into the long driveway and looked at King with a worried expression in her eyes. He'd ridden the entire trip without speaking a word.

He blinked, looked up with a startled expression, and then wearily wiped his hands across his burning eyes.

"How am I going to tell everyone?" he muttered. "What do I say? Oh, by the way, Duncan is dead now? He hated me so much that when his plan to get even failed, he shot himself?"

"King," Jesse rebuked softly. "It's not your fault. Nor is it mine. I could be sitting here telling myself that if I'd loved him, instead of you, you'd both be alive. The world does not run on 'what ifs.'"

King glanced sideways at Jesse, grimaced, and then opened the door.

"I'll tell Maggie, I'll find the words…somehow."

"We'll tell her together, King," she replied, as she walked beside him toward the house. She slipped her hand in his and squeezed gently. "We'll tell them *all* together."

Somehow the deed had been accomplished. Uttering the words aloud had, in some way, increased the horror. But the telling was over. Now all they had to do was bury Duncan and get on with their lives. It was easier said than done.

It was late as Maggie bid good night and finally departed to her bedroom for a much needed rest. Jesse walked through the house, moving quietly on bare feet as she checked the locks on the doors. This was usually something King did, but not tonight. Jesse knew a nightly routine would be the last thing on his mind.

The memorial service had been disastrous. How could one mourn the loss of a stranger? That's what Duncan had become. All Jesse had been able to do was say a prayer, hoping he'd find a peace that had escaped him in life elsewhere. She hadn't known what King was thinking during the services. He'd remained too silent, watching it all from a distance, not allowing himself to grieve in any manner. As soon as they'd come home, King shut himself in the den...away from phone calls...away from sympathy or pity.

But it was late, and Jesse had worried herself into tomorrow. King had had enough time alone. She was going in, and she wasn't taking no for an answer.

She opened the door and stood silently in the doorway, allowing her eyes to adjust to the darkness inside.

"Close the door."

King's voice came out of the shadows and Jesse stepped inside, complying with his gruff order.

"Where are you?" Jesse asked softly, and started to turn on the lamp beside the door when another order in the form of a plea stopped her hand.

"Don't turn on the light, please."

Jesse followed the sound of his voice to the long, overstuffed leather sofa in the middle of the room. She stopped as her foot touched the corner, walked around behind the sofa, and traced her hand along the cushions and down the side until she felt the uneven rise and fall of King's bare chest.

"Sweetheart," Jesse said, and then felt King clutch at her hands in desperation.

"Come here," he coaxed, as he reached upward, pulling Jesse gently off her feet and over the back of the sofa until she lay stretched full length on top of him.

He clasped her face in his hands and ran the tips of his thumbs carefully along the line of her cheeks down to the corners of her mouth, before he pulled her into his kiss with a low, hungry groan.

He drank from the comfort of Jesse's touch, seeking solace from her taste just as he'd sought solace from the empty glass and half-empty bottle on the floor beside the sofa. Neither took away the slow burn inside his belly.

Finally he released Jesse's mouth and buried his face in her hair.

"I can't make it go away," King whispered hoarsely. "I can't even get drunk. Help me, Jesse Rose. Just help me get through tonight."

King felt her tears fall in sparse sprinkles on his face and neck, as her mouth captured the sun-tanned skin on his body in sharp, hungry bites. She moved silently over him, feeling with every caress of her fingers the growing urgency and need in his body.

King yearned for Jesse in a way he'd never imagined

possible. Tonight, they both needed to be reminded of life—death had been too near.

King lay still, a willing victim of Jesse's tender mercies. When he heard her removing her clothing in the thick darkness, he quickly followed suit.

Suddenly there was no time for pretense, no time left to wait for the passion to build. Urgency took away what was left of will power as King took Jesse into his arms in one powerful motion, and drove his hard, aching body into her sweet warmth with a desperate thrust.

The sensation was devastating. Every muscle in Jesse's body tensed and then pulsed around and on King. She felt him begin to shudder, heard the harsh gasps for breath as he thrust into her again and again.

Tiny moans slipped between their mouths as Jesse took King's breath and traded it for her own. Her hands clasped tightly behind his neck as her legs wrapped around his waist, pulling him deeper and deeper into the only solace she could provide.

Release came suddenly in the form of a white-hot flash of pleasure that sent them both falling backward onto the sofa in weak relief.

Jesse sat straddling his lap, as King buried his face in the gentle swell of her breasts beneath his searching hands. She felt the tension flowing from his shoulders and his heartbeat kick into a lower rhythm as all sense of desperation and urgency passed in the quiet darkness.

"I love you, King McCandless," Jesse whispered as

she gently brushed the damp locks of his hair from his forehead.

King sighed softly and pulled her into a fierce hug of thanksgiving. He just wished he could love himself. Maybe then this awful, growing guilt would disappear and he could love Jesse back the way she deserved to be loved.

The following week was a nightmare Jesse feared would never end. It began with continuous phone calls, most from old friends, some from journalists, looking for a new angle to an old story.

The more confusion that erupted, the further King withdrew. He didn't communicate with anyone unless he had to. Even Jesse suffered from his long bouts of moody silence. She knew he'd eventually come to realize none of this had been his fault, but it would take time. Nothing she nor anyone said now was getting through to him. He needed time. She was going to give it to him.

She had to go back to St. Louis and tie up the loose ends of her old life. She was ready for a new one.

"Maggie," Jesse called down the hallway, "is Turner outside yet?"

"No, honey. But he should be here soon. Need any help?"

"No," she answered, and dashed breathlessly into the living room where Maggie stood watching for her ride to the airport. "I'm just taking an overnight bag. I don't plan on being gone more than a day...two at the most. I'll spend the night with my friend Sheila, and use the day to finalize my errands. I'll be home before you know I'm gone.''

"I already miss you, honey," Maggie said, hugging Jesse quickly, then returning to her vigilant post as lookout for Turner and his pickup truck.

Jesse had tried several times over the last few days to talk to King. She wanted to tell him about her need to go back to St. Louis for a short time. She had a buyer for her house, and needed to see her principal at the school and get an official release from her teaching contract.

But each time she broached the subject, King would plead an urgent duty or totally ignore her efforts to get close. He wouldn't touch her except in the most casual of manners. It was as if their time together had never existed. Jesse was staying in her own room again, alone and frustrated at King's refusal to share his sorrow with anyone. He wouldn't even admit he felt sorrow, when in fact he was utterly miserable.

"He's here!" Maggie called. And, before she knew it, Jesse was gone. She had a feeling that when King came home tonight, he wasn't going to like this one bit.

A long, hungry rumble accompanied the clouds darkening the sky over Tulsa. Maggie looked anxiously out the window and muttered, "Lord, if you're just teasing, stop it right now. We've needed rain too long to be disappointed again."

But the thunder continued, and the sky got darker and darker. Maybe this time it was finally going to rain.

King hammered the last nail in place in the big gate separating the house and cattle pastures. His muscles ached, his blue chambray work shirt had a three-cornered tear Maggie was going to fuss about, and the perspiration had plastered his Levi's to his long legs with stubborn stickiness. He was tired, dirty, and hadn't felt this good in weeks. Maybe when he got home this evening, he could talk Jesse into going out for dinner, that is, if she was still talking to him.

He knew he'd been uncommunicative. He knew he should have been able to talk to Jesse, but somehow he just couldn't. He felt so responsible for what had happened to her, and he kept remembering how he'd wanted to kill the man who'd hurt her. No matter what his brain kept telling him, his heart told him differently. Duncan was dead, and he'd watched it happen.

But over the past few days, being back at the ranch and working long, hot hours either with the men or alone, he'd begun to heal.

Thunder rumbled across the sky. He looked up in surprise. He hadn't noticed the air cooling, or the sky darkening. He whistled for Tariq, who was grazing aimlessly along the fence line, and watched with admiration as the beautiful animal jerked his head up and answered his call on the run.

"Come on, boy," King murmured, as he slipped his

tool belt into the saddle bag. "We better get off this hill before we fry."

He wasn't anxious to be a target for the lightning he saw in the gathering clouds. "Let's go home."

King made it to the house just ahead of the first deluge. The clouds opened and literally poured water onto the arid land. The drought was over.

"Where's Jesse?" King asked, as he wandered back to the kitchen where a very stern Maggie was preparing the evening meal.

"Gone," she announced shortly. She, too, was irked at King's continuing silences. If he'd listened, he would have known where Jesse had gone.

King felt the floor tilt beneath him. A dull, aching throb began behind his eyelids. He could barely speak.

"Where?" he asked softly.

"St. Louis," Maggie replied. "She tried to tell you for three days, but you were too busy to listen. It couldn't wait any longer."

"She left me?" King whispered, and sank down to the bar stool behind him.

Maggie relented at the look of utter desolation on King's face. He'd suffered enough the last few days to last a lifetime.

"She'll be back," Maggie said, and walked over to King. "Come here, boy," she said softly. "I need a hug."

King felt her arms go around his neck as she pulled his head down on her ample shoulder.

"I'm sorry," he said, past the ache in his throat. He

relished the familiar comfort, yet the empty spot in his heart continued to grow wider. He fiercely returned her hug.

"I'm not the one you need to be saying that to, mister," Maggie said. She planted a swift kiss on his cheek, then turned and busied herself back at the sink. She didn't want him to see her cry.

Maggie needn't have worried. King couldn't have seen her tears for the ones blinding him. He walked slowly out of the house and stood beneath the shelter of the porch as the rain continued to fall, washing the trees and the land clean from the long months of stifling dust and heat, as it washed the last remnants of guilt from King's soul. He watched the day end with a promise in his heart of a better tomorrow.

"I need a one-way ticket to St. Louis," King growled. He couldn't believe he was actually getting back on a damn airplane. But it was the fastest way to get to Jesse.

"Yes, sir," the lady behind the ticket counter replied. "Moving, are you?"

"No!" King answered, ignoring the curious look on the woman's face.

"Have you checked your baggage?" she asked, stamping his ticket, then handing it back across the counter.

"Don't have any," King said shortly, then glared, daring her to continue her nosy harangue. "I'm coming back today."

"Then you'll want a round-trip ticket," she announced, and started to pull the ticket away.

"No, I don't," he argued, and stuffed the ticket in his pocket. "This is the last time I willingly get on an airplane. I'm coming home today. If I have to, I'll buy a car, but I won't get back on another damn tin bird."

He walked away, already dreading the sick sensation of lifting off the ground and the feeling of being out-of-control. Jesse better know how much he loved her, because he wouldn't be able to do much more than shake when he arrived.

Jesse folded the last of the clothes she intended to take back to Tulsa, and piled the rest in a stack headed for Goodwill.

The painters had done a good job of cleaning up her bedroom, yet she could hardly bring herself to stay long enough in it to get her belongings. Too many bad memories hung heavily in the air. Her principal was more than happy to release her from her contract. The certified substitute he hired had proven to be a good teacher. It was going to work out nicely all around.

Jesse said goodbye to her friend Sheila, made promises to visit, and breathed a sigh of relief. Now all she had to do was load her car and she would be on her way home…to King. When she got back, if she had to, she'd kidnap *him* until he stopped this foolish silence. King was just going to have to learn how to share more than his body with her. She smiled a slow, secretive smile, and thought to herself, *But, his body was a good place to start the sharing process. We'll take it from there.*

She worked in comfortable silence until the ringing doorbell interrupted her progress. Assuming that it was probably Goodwill coming to pick up her clothing donation, she got the shock of her life when a man's large shadow loomed in the doorway.

"King!" Jesse cried. "Honey, are you all right?"

The look of desolation in his eyes scared her silly. Had something else happened? She was almost afraid to ask as she pulled him by the arm into her house.

"You left me," he accused in a husky voice.

Jesse breathed a relieved sigh, threw her arms around him in a boisterous welcome, then began kissing his shirt front. It was as far as she could reach.

"Didn't Maggie tell you?" Jesse asked, as she cupped his face in her hands. "I tried to, but you wouldn't listen…and this couldn't wait."

King closed his eyes, turning his face into the palm of her hand, tracing her lifeline with the tip of his tongue, then grabbed her roughly and pulled her off the floor.

"Jesse," he whispered against her lips. "I'm so sorry, baby, I know I should have been able to talk…especially to you. But somehow it got all twisted up in my head. I felt like it was my fault. It took days for that feeling to lessen. I need you to make it go away."

"Sweetheart," she murmured, and brushed her mouth softly across his lips. "You already have me.

You didn't need to follow me here. You should have known I'd be back.''

King watched the love in her eyes grow, and felt a healing warmth flow between them.

"I love you so much, Jesse Rose."

"I love you, too, King. But you should have trusted me. I wouldn't leave you...not again."

"I know that, baby," he said gruffly.

"Then why are you here?" Jesse asked, as King lifted her into his arms.

"I'm just doing what I should have done three years ago, Jesse Rose. I've come to take you home."

* * * * *

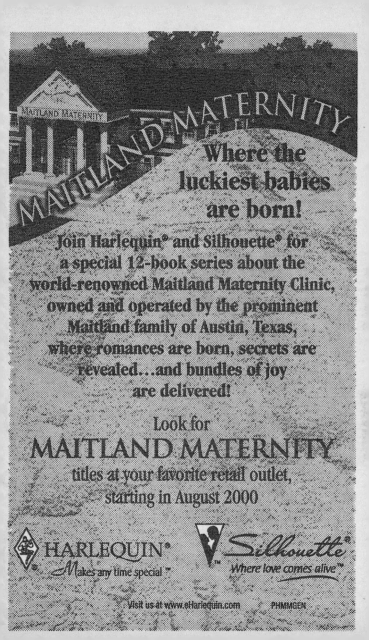

Silhouette invites you to come back to Whitehorn, Montana...

MONTANA MAVERICKS

WED IN WHITEHORN—
12 BRAND-NEW stories that capture living and loving beneath the Big Sky where legends live on and love lasts forever!

MM

And the adventure continues...

February 2001—
Jennifer Mikels *Rich, Rugged...Ruthless* (#9)

March 2001—
Cheryl St.John *The Magnificent Seven* (#10)

April 2001—
Laurie Paige *Outlaw Marriage* (#11)

May 2001—
Linda Turner *Nighthawk's Child* (#12)

Available at your favorite retail outlet.

Silhouette®
Where love comes alive™

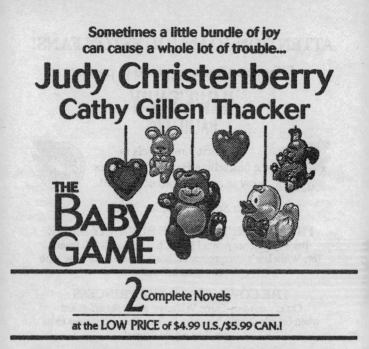

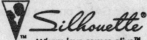